Who has Poisoned the Sea?

Books by
AUDREY COPPARD

FICTION

Who Has Poisoned the Sea?
This Could be the Start of Something

NON-FICTION

Sending Secrets

Audrey Coppard

Who has Poisoned the Sea?

Illustrated by
Douglas Phillips

HEINEMANN : LONDON

William Heinemann Ltd
15 Queen Street, Mayfair, London W1X 8BE
LONDON MELBOURNE TORONTO
JOHANNESBURG AUCKLAND

First published 1970
Reprinted 1971, 1973
© Audrey Coppard 1970
Illustrations © William Heinemann Ltd 1970
434 93300 7

Reproduced and Printed in Great Britain by
Redwood Press Limited
Trowbridge, Wiltshire

I

Sunday at Home

Tim Dunwoodie looked round the door of his mother's bedroom for the seventh time that morning.

'When will lunch be ready?' he asked plaintively.

'Drat it, Tim, can't you forget your stomach for two minutes on end?' Her voice was muffled by a mouth full of pins. 'Can't you see how busy we are?'

He could indeed. Tess and Pauline were trying on pink bridesmaids' dresses. Ellen was perched on the bed, busily sewing. His fourth sister, the bride-to-be, was being pinned into an ocean of white veil by his mother, who knelt in the foam of it, flustered and hot.

'Only three more weeks,' she sighed, 'and I'll never get half of it done in time.'

'You will, mum,' Ellen said soothingly.

Tess was turning this way and that in front of the wardrobe mirror.

'Do you think it makes me look fat?'

'Yes,' Tim said, disgusted, and went downstairs again. He counted the pennies he had in his pocket, and left the house.

It was only a short walk to the village sweetshop. He pushed open the door and somewhere a buzzer sounded.

Old Mrs Nelson appeared behind the counter. 'What'll

you have? Quick!' she asked. 'I'm up to my elbows in pastry.'

The whole world seemed too busy that morning to spare him a moment, Tim thought morosely. He looked down the High Street, sucking a toffee. Cars were streaming by, all in one direction. Normancote, where Tim lived, was on the main road, four miles inland from a resort on the Kent coast. On fine Sunday mornings such as this, a thousand cars an hour rushed through the village and in the evening rushed back again. None of them ever stopped. Normancote did not have anything picturesque about it. There was a cluster of houses round a nondescript church, and a small housing estate, where the Dunwoodies lived, which had been described by somebody in the local paper as an 'infernal eyesore'.

Tim's friend, Victor, came cycling up the street and waved. He waved back.

'Coming out this afternoon, Vic?'

'Can't. We've got people coming.'

'My place is like a madhouse. Everyone's trying on dresses.'

'What, for the wedding?'

'Yep. Lousy sisters.'

Victor made a rude noise in sympathy and then cycled off.

Tim did not really feel gloomy. It was a lovely morning, and there was still a week of the summer holidays left before he went back to school.

A lunch of sorts was being prepared when he got home again.

'You'll have to amuse yourself this afternoon, dear,' his mother said. 'You don't mind, do you?'

'No, that's OK.'

'What will you do?'

'Oh, I'll go for a walk. Up on the hill, I think.'

He meant the high ridge that separated Normancote from the sea.

His mother nodded, satisfied. 'Take some food with you. Then you can have a picnic and I won't have to bother with your tea. The dresses are nowhere near finished.'

Tim often went off for walks on his own. Perhaps it was because he had so little privacy at home, but from an early age he had enjoyed wandering off and exploring the countryside around his village. On one such walk, he had found a hollow, right at the top of the hill overlooking the sea. In the hollow there were wild flowers and butterflies, protected from the wind. Around it, a few small elder trees and bramble bushes grew, giving it a covered, secret air. And he called it his Secret Dell and told no one about it except his grandfather.

The old man had been fixing a hook on his fishing rod when he mentioned the Dell.

'I found a hollow, right up on top of the hill there. It's got bushes growing round it.'

Grandfather looked up, interested. 'I know the place. That's where a plane crashed during the war.'

'A plane? You mean it made that big hole?'

'That's right. I remember going up there to see the wreck with your grandma. It was one of our own, come down in the Battle of Britain.'

After that the Dell seemed even more mysterious. Tim searched and searched but never found any sign of a plane, not even a little piece of metal.

On this particular Sunday it was warm and quiet, with just the hum of insects and the wind rustling the bushes

3

as it swept in from the sea. Tim picked some early black-berries which made his eyes water, they were so sour. Out at sea, great cloud shapes massed in towers of grey and gold, driven by the rising wind, but in his Secret Dell it was warm and protected. Careful not to lie on a thistle, he lay stretched out and, without trying, soon fell asleep.

2

The Meeting with Percy

Tim woke up with a start. A fly had landed on his ear and the humming had mingled with a dream all about planes flying low overhead, in from the sea, chasing each other and firing guns. He scratched his ear and yawned. His father had told him something of the Battle of Britain, and how brave the young pilots had been, but to Tim the war seemed very unreal and far away. Once he had told his Grandfather the Dell made him feel a little bit frightened because the pilot of the plane had died there.

'Don't be daft. England is so old, there can't be many places where someone or other hasn't died at some time. Take this cottage. Your grandma died here, and old Tom Tupper before her, and the Goodwins before that. But it ain't a bit creepy, is it?'

In the Dell it had suddenly turned very cold. Tim shivered and wished he had brought a jumper. The clouds were greyer and nearer now.

'Brr,' he said aloud to himself, 'it's *freezing*.'

Someone was watching him. He knew it, even before he turned round. Someone was standing behind him, looking over the edge of the Dell.

He turned quickly and felt the hairs on the back of his neck rise with fear.

5

There was someone there. Someone with a bald head. On the pink scalp where hair should have been were blue, metallic-looking knobs, shining faintly in the afternoon sun. And what made the sight really frightening was the fact that the bald head belonged to a young boy.

He was leaning over the edge of the hollow, staring fixedly at Tim, who sat, frozen with fear, at the bottom. Because he had been thinking about the dead pilot, his first thought was that this was his ghost. But somehow, even while he was thinking it, he knew it was not.

The boy looked about the same age as Tim. He was wearing a short tunic of some sort of grey material, with long trousers and shoes all in one, like a pair of tights. And the strange, metallic shapes on his head.

If Tim had not been so frightened, he would have been aware that the other boy was just as frightened as he was.

He tried opening his mouth to shout or scream, but no sound came. There was silence for a full ten seconds, and then the boy spoke.

'I . . . I come in peace,' he said, his voice squeaking a little with nervousness. 'Where on earth am I?'

Tim still could not speak. His tongue was stuck to the roof of his mouth, but the boy's words had set his thoughts racing. This was no ghost. He was too young to be the ghost of the dead pilot and, anyway, he was far too real-looking. Tim's next thought was that the earth had been invaded from outer space. He certainly was a weird-looking boy, with those knobs on his head. And yet he had spoken in English, and had asked where on *earth* he was.

The boy in grey spoke again. 'Hairy one, where am I?'

Hairy one! Tim swallowed and found he was able to reply: 'Normancote. In K-Kent.'

The stranger frowned, and looked all about him. One of the attachments on his head glowed faintly. Then he turned and spoke again.

'I am very perplexed. Normancote is where I am supposed to be. Yet everything looks so—different.'

He started to walk down into the hollow, which made Tim huddle instinctively in a defensive way.

'Where is the University?'

Tim stared. 'There isn't a university. I mean, d-do you think you've got the right place?'

7

The boy snorted in a very human way, then shrugged.

'All I know is, I got off the airtrack at four o'clock to walk to the University.' He held out his hands in a curiously helpless gesture. 'I've got to get there right away for my history tests.'

Tim looked wildly about him at the bare hill. 'What university are you on about?'

'The one at Normancote, of course.' He looked round at the hill also, and again gave a helpless gesture with his hands.

Tim had another, more frightening thought. Perhaps he was a madman, an escaped lunatic. There was a big mental hospital not very far away. He had heard of one or two people escaping. Sometimes they could be quite dangerous.

As if he could sense Tim's new fears, the strange boy turned and gave a friendly smile.

'Please don't be frightened,' he said. 'Something very strange has happened to us both. We must try to understand it.'

Tim nodded and gave a sickly grin. 'Yes,' he said brightly. 'Understand it.' If he *was* an escaped lunatic, the best thing to do was humour him.

'I was walking down the hill,' the boy was explaining, 'when one of my microcybs seemed to go wrong. I tried to mend it, knocked a wire off my telecyb, and then everything went cold and—different.'

'Are those micro—whatever you said?' Tim just had to ask, pointing at the knobs on the boy's head.

'Don't you *know*? Where's your set?'

Tim shook his head, and gave another sickly grin. Two of the knobs were glowing again faintly. The boy stood, considering Tim and the Dell.

8

'Tell me,' he suddenly said. 'What is the date?'

'Now I'm sure he's daft,' Tim thought, getting up on his feet ready to run. But he said the date, slowly and clearly, edging towards the other side of the hollow as he did so.

The boy in grey started to cry out as Tim told him, and his eyes filled with a strange horror.

'But this is awful! What has happened? When I walked down the road, it was the 28th of August, A.D. 2469.'

There was a shocked silence while they both considered this. Then the boy added, despairingly. 'Somehow I've projected myself backwards in time for five hundred years! Oh, *drat* these microcybs!'

3
Percy

'Now whatever shall I do?' the boy said dejectedly.

Tim said nothing. His strongest wish at that moment was to run down the hill as fast as possible. He was shaking.

'Please don't run away.'

Tim jumped. The boy was looking at him strangely. But he stayed where he was.

'I think my telecyb is beginning to work. If you stay quiet, and try not to be frightened, I think we shall see into each other's minds.'

'All right,' Tim stammered, still sure the boy was mad.

'Shall we tell names?' he was asking, a little shyly. 'My name is Percy.'

'Mine's Tim Dunwoodie.' In the silence that followed, he tried to master the panic that welled up inside him. He stopped shaking. Then a curious thing happened: the other boy's mind rose up and seemed to enter his own. All his fear melted away. Percy was no longer a frightening a stranger, a madman. He *knew* him. Their minds met and explored each other. He knew Percy was kind, and frightened, and much more clever than he was. They smiled at each other and sat down at the bottom of the Dell.

'So you are real? And not mad?'

'I thought the same of you!'

They both laughed, relief flooding them, making them want to talk.

'But how can you be here? I mean, these things you wear can't make it happen, can they?'

'Well, I've never heard of it happening before. It must have been a combination of things going wrong. But I can only draw tentative conclusions from insufficient data.'

Tim scratched his head, puzzled. 'Do you mean—guess?'

'That is a strange word to me.'

'Oh. I think it means the same as what you said.'

Percy continued, 'All I know is what I have already told you. I was walking towards the University across Campus Hill,' he gestured around him, 'and I stopped to adjust my history microcyb because it felt a bit loose. I knocked a wire out of my telecyb, and it must have got tangled up. Anyway, they're not working properly now.' He touched his head.

Tim sat, trying to believe this wonderful thing was really happening to him. Because he could see into his mind, he knew Percy was telling him the truth. He could feel his curiosity, and wonder. And right at the back of Percy's mind, he could sense some ever-present pain, something large and deep.

'Percy. That's a funny name. To me, that is.'

Percy looked surprised. 'Is it? I have been told it is a very old, very honourable English name.'

Tim could not disagree. 'Those things on your head, those knobs. They make you look—well, you look awful.'

He hoped he had not hurt Percy's feelings, saying this,

and was relieved to 'see' he had not.

'If your time doesn't have them and you've never seen them before, I suppose they do. I must say you look odd to me, with all that hair.'

Tim put out a finger, not quite daring to touch one of the microcybs. 'How do they work?'

'Do you know about computers?'

When Tim nodded, he went on, 'Ah, yes. They were just beginning in your time. Well, these are computers of a sort. It's more sensible to carry them around with you, and they work better when they are linked with human reasoning. It's a convenient way of taking knowledge around with you, that's all.'

'You said your history one had gone wrong. Does that mean you have a different one for different things?'

'Roughly. They have certain information in each, attached to the correct part of the brain by impulses, sort of electrical, do you understand? It's a bit complicated.'

Tim was sure of that. There were still a million questions he wanted to ask, but his mind was too full of what he had already learned.

Now Percy was asking a question. 'What are your clothes made of?'

Tim looked. 'Oh, all sorts. This is cotton. This is wool and nylon, I think.'

'Forgive me mentioning it, but they seem to absorb dirt.'

He looked down at his shorts and shirt. Certainly they could have been cleaner.

'What are yours made of, then?'

'Perfilx.' Percy saw that the word was new to Tim and added, 'It has only been in use about 200 years. The material cleans itself by sort of molecular vibration.'

'Oh. Anything else strange about me?'

Percy considered for a moment. 'Nothing visual, except the hair. Surprisingly little, really.'

Then Tim thought of a new thing. 'If you've got telepathy knobs on your head, why do we have to talk?'

'I can't read your thoughts. Only your feelings, with a telecyb. It has no intellectual function.'

Tim struggled to understand. 'You mean, we can only tell things about each other, like, are we friendly towards each other, or are we frightened of each other?'

'Yes, that's it. But it does more, lots more. For instance, it indicates falsity.'

'I think I know what you mean. It's like a lie detector.'

Percy nodded. 'Except no one tells lies any more. There is no point.'

That was one use of telepathy that had never occurred to Tim. His head was swimming with excitement and all the fresh ideas.

'To think I thought you mad when we first met!'

Percy looked serious. 'Madness? There used to be a lot of madness in the world. But now with the telecybs, we can help.'

'How do you mean?'

'You surround a sick mind with a group of healthy ones, who try and understand the sickness. Then the sick person is calmed, and no longer feels alone. Then the doctors can quickly establish what is wrong and cure it.'

Tim looked a little bewildered. 'I don't really understand everything you say, but you make the future sound a wonderful time.'

'We have solved some problems. We have others in their place . . .' His voice trailed off with a sigh. Again Tim was aware of the pain at the back of Percy's mind.

13

Percy seemed to shrug off his troubles, whatever they were. 'But tell me about *you*,' he said. 'If I've gone back into history, I might as well use the time to my own advantage and discover something from the mistake. When—or I should say, *if*—I get back to my own time, I'll know much more for my history examination if you tell me about life in Normancote 500 years ago.'

Tim looked doubtful. 'What sort of things do you want to know?'

'Well, let's start with you and your family. What sort of house you live in, what your father does for a living, that sort of thing.'

Tim drew a deep breath. 'I don't know what Normancote is like in your time, but right now it's just a village. People do farming and work in shops. There's a factory a few miles away. My father travels around the area, selling tractors and farm machinery.'

He stopped. He felt shy, as he never liked talking about himself or his family. 'Is that the sort of thing?'

'Yes, yes. Do please go on. What about the rest of your family?'

'My mum looks after us—there's me and four sisters.'

Percy looked surprised. 'What a big family! You are very lucky.'

'Lucky?' Tim practically choked. 'They're horrible! At least, Ellen isn't too bad, she's just a bit older than me. But the others—well, Vivian, that's the oldest, she's getting married soon and you never saw such a fuss. All they do is talk about dresses and flowers and shoes until I could be sick. Pauline works in a hairdresser's, and Tess at a nursery. Not a baby nursery, a garden nursery.'

Percy interrupted. 'Hairdressers? Women have their hair dressed?'

'I suppose women are bald in your time?' The thought was somehow horrible. He tried to imagine all his sisters bald.

'Anyway, that's us. We live down there.' He pointed towards the village. 'It's on a new housing estate, not very big. But we've got central heating.'

'What's the house made of?'

'Tiles, bricks, cement, you know, things like that.'

Percy looked as surprised as if Tim had told him he lived in a cave.

'We've got electricity and television and telephones and things,' he finished off, a little lamely. He hoped Percy wasn't going to ask him any really difficult questions about things like politics. To tell the truth, he was not even quite sure who the Prime Minister was, or how the Houses of Parliament worked. He knew the country was always being told to produce more and import less, but he never gave much thought to such matters.

But Percy seemed still to be thinking about the family.

'I wish I had a brother or a sister. Some people on the earth have two children, and in the space colonies they can have as many as they like, of course.'

'Space colonies? Do you mean people live on the stars?' Tim was almost shouting with excitement.

'Of course. Well, on planets, actually. But it isn't a very exciting life. The work is very dull and hard, and only people like geologists and miners go to live there.'

'And what about people from outer space?' Tim could hardly bring himself to ask. 'Are there any other beings in outer space?'

'None that I know of. So far as we have found out, we are the only people in the universe.' He laughed. 'Don't look so disappointed!'

They talked together for a long while, asking each other questions, putting forward ideas. Tim told Percy about cars and rockets and his school, and about money.

'I can't imagine how this will help you with your history exam,' he finished up.

'It will, though. This is the sort of social history I need. Microcybs tell of things like wars and kings and trade, but they don't tell what kind of television programmes people watched, or how many children are in a class.'

'I'm on holiday from school still. But we go back next week.' Tim paused. It seemed ridiculous to be saying 'next week' to somebody who lived 500 years from now.

Percy was thinking of something else, and spoke in a dreamy way. 'This is a sort of miracle, isn't it? More than a dream. It is quite outside anything we both know as normal, and yet we have to accept it.'

'It's like a dream to me. I keep feeling as if I'm going to wake up.'

'In some ways I wish it were a dream. Then I would not have to worry about getting back to my own time.'

Percy made his expressive gesture that Tim thought very beautiful and graceful. He never used his own hands like that.

'But while I am still here, let's talk some more about you. You were saying you are on holiday?'

'Yes. We've just come back from two weeks in Exmouth.'

'Exmouth? That is in Devon, isn't it?'

Tim noticed that Percy sounded a little bit strange.

'What did you do there?'

'The usual. I've got a new fishing rod, and Dad and I did some fishing. We swam and went on a boat. Picnicked on the beach. *You* know.'

Percy was not looking at him. The pain that Tim had sensed at the back of all they said to each other suddenly flared up in the boy's brain, and hit him as if the pain were a blow.

Percy spoke, almost mumbled. 'No, I don't know. We do not do those things now, in my time. We can no longer go swimming, or fish, or even walk on the beach. The sea is a terrible, horrible place and we dare not go near. In my time, the sea is poisoned.'

4

The Poisoned Sea

'Poisoned? The whole sea?' Tim was shaken and unbelieving. 'You can't poison a whole sea!'

Percy nodded sorrowfully, helplessly. 'You can, or someone can. Someone *has*. Well, nearly all the seas, and it's spreading. We don't know what the poison is, that's the terrible thing about it, and all we can do is guess. All we know is, it starts in the middle of the Atlantic, and it is new, and quite deadly.'

Tim looked at his friend's unhappy face. He was shaken by the strength of his pain. 'That is what is making you so sad. I could feel it all along,' he said gently.

'Yes.'

They sat quietly together, and Tim waited for Percy to go on. As if it could hold the answer, they both turned to look out to sea. It was no longer sparkling, but looked grey and heavy under the advancing clouds.

'It did not start too long ago. Only about five years. Up until then, the sea was just like it's always been. At first the scientists thought it was atomic waste. That still crops up from time to time. Then they thought it was coming up from inside the earth itself. But it wasn't. They got more and more frightened, because it seemed to be some sort of chain reaction, constantly growing. It can't be stopped. It kills the fish, and every form of life in the sea wherever it goes.'

The pain seared and burned. Tim could hardly bear it.

Percy went on in the same flat tone. 'My family also live near the sea. Like most people who can, we own a pet dolphin. I've had mine since I was five. He's part of the family . . .'

Tim hardly dared ask. 'Is he—is he dead?'

'No. He lives in a tank in our garden now. But he is very sick, the poison has got into him. And as no one knows what it is, we can't make him well. And he pines for the sea and his friends. He will certainly die.'

So that was it. That was the desperate sorrow that Percy could not hide. Once Tim had owned a guinea-pig and it had died. He had cried about it, but knew he had felt nothing like the pain and love that Percy felt for his dolphin.

'Do you think your scientists will find out soon?'

'They are working on it, day and night,' Percy replied in a steadier voice. 'It's not just the fish and the dolphins. You see, the poison is spreading to places like the Indian Ocean, and around there people rely on fish for their food. There are all sorts of ocean-bed farming going on there, too. All that will have to stop, and thousands of people may starve.'

The part that seemed most real to Tim was the dolphin.

Percy was trying to smile. 'I can't remember if you have pet dolphins in your time.'

'No, not really. I've heard of places where they are trained to play with balls and do tricks.'

'Ah, it's coming soon, then. They really are very intelligent, you know. Much more than other animals.'

19

'What can they do?'

'Heaps of things. They can take messages to the ocean-bed farms. They mend damaged cables. They tell us where to find the most fish. Apart from being such fun. My dolphin, he's called Beppo, taught me to swim and dive and love the sea.'

'That's his name, then, Beppo.' Tim tried to speak in sympathy. 'You make him sound such fun. Honestly, I know how you feel.'

Percy could sense his new friend's feeling, of course, and he smiled. 'You would love to have a dolphin like Beppo, I know. Of course, they can't talk, but we understand a lot of their movements and language. And lately some of the cleverest ones, like Beppo, have taken to wearing telecybs.'

'Those knobs!' Tim spluttered.

'They do look so funny,' Percy laughed. 'Especially the ones who carry satchels.'

'Satchels?'

'They carry them when they take messages under the sea. Beppo didn't do that. But when he was wearing his telecyb, it was almost as good as talking to each other. He is so intelligent. We knew what gave each other pleasure and he would do the things he knew made me laugh. I could feel his illness coming on, too. After a while, when the pain got to be bad, I couldn't bear it. I took his telecyb off.'

They sat in silence. Then Percy said, 'Did you know the dolphins can dance?'

It was too much for Tim. Dancing dolphins, wearing satchels and knobs on their heads. 'You're joking.'

'No, I'm not. It's true. Listen, Beppo took me on his back one day to watch it for myself. Right out at sea. It was a sort of story, a ritual dance. It is one of their ways of communicating with each other, because their squeaks don't really make up a language.'

'Well, I won't believe it until *I* see it.'

Percy smiled. 'Then you never will. At least, I think you live too long ago.'

'It's as much as I can do to believe in *you*.'

'I know.'

'The fantastic thing is, we are speaking to each other. I mean, although you wear telecybs and things, you aren't all that much different from me, are you?'

Percy shook his head. 'But the world has gone through some very strange times between your and my time. We have had to make life a lot simpler, much more like it used to be, otherwise there probably would be no people left at all. I don't think I should tell you all about it. I think somehow I shouldn't tell you too much. But we are living in what is known as the Age of Simplification.'

'Oh. But do all the people wear microcybs? Or just some?'

'Most people. There are a few who do not. They are the ones we call Elders. They do not wear them because they no longer need to. No one can be quite sure why, or what has happened to their brains, but they are changing into a new type of human being. It's nothing to be frightened of, though. They are beautiful people. Probably it is the way all human minds will go in a few hundred years. They can read each other's minds without telecybs. In lots of ways they are different.'

'Can't *they* tell you what poisoned the sea?'

'Not yet. I suppose if anyone can find out what it is, they will.'

'Are they your leaders?'

'No. They have no function. They are just ordinary people to begin with, and when they find out their brains are developing, they go to live together, very simply. Anyone can ask their advice if they want to, of course.'

'I wish I could help find out about the poison.'

'Some scientists think it may have started about your time. They think it has taken a long time to change into what it is. I just don't know.'

The sat, quietly, comfortably, like old friends. It could not last. Already Percy was thinking about how to return. He looked at the sky. The sun had shifted and now was hidden by the banking clouds. It was late afternoon.

'Well, it looks as if I have missed the examinations,' Percy sighed. 'Whatever shall I use as an excuse?'

Tim said nothing. He was thinking it would be hard for Percy to get back to his own time to make any kind of excuse at all. He looked at the microcybs.

'When you do go, Percy, I don't suppose we shall ever meet again.'

They both felt sad. 'It isn't likely.' Percy gave one of his beautiful gestures. 'I came by a series of errors, and I think it would be impossible to repeat them. But what worries me is how to reverse the process, and go back.'

Tim realized suddenly how brave Percy was being.

'Do you know, if it had been me, I would have just sat screaming for help. I wouldn't have asked lots of questions like you have.'

'That's not true. You are better than that. I can tell that, given half a chance, you would come back to my time with me.' Percy smiled kindly. 'And that shows you're braver than you think.'

It was true. Tim realized that, for quite a time, he had been thinking how marvellous it would be to enter Percy's world for a little while, just as the boy had entered his.

Percy was trying to untwist some wires on his head.

'When our television set goes wrong, a good bash on the side always gets it going again,' Tim ventured to say. 'At least, that's what my dad always does, and it seems to work.'

Percy was laughing at him. 'No wonder you are known to use as the Age of Amateurs! Somehow I don't think that kind of behaviour works with microcybs.'

Tim felt hurt. At once Percy reacted to his mood.

'All the same, I'll try it. No harm done if I give them a little shake.'

He did so, and laughed at Tim again. 'There, I . . .'

He was gone. Tim could see nothing of him. The Dell, the hill, the sky, everything was as it had been before, except he was now on his own. The air suddenly felt warmer than before, full of a clammy heat. From out at sea, he heard the rumble of thunder.

Tim got shakily to his feet, and looked about him, just to make sure Percy was not there.

Then he stumbled down the hill towards his home.

5

The Storm

'You look pale as a ghost.' It was Ellen who first noticed Tim. He was standing just inside the kitchen, leaning against the wall. His eyes looked black and large with delayed shock. He tried to speak, but no words would come out properly.

'I . . . I . . .' he stammered.

Ellen put an arm round her young brother and began to look really concerned.

'What's wrong?'

He allowed himself to be led across to a chair, and the familiar, warm smell of the kitchen, with its ticking clock and his family all about, helped to calm him.

'Whatever's wrong?' His mother, who saw that something was wrong, came and bent over him, feeling his forehead as she did so. It felt clammy and cold. 'Have you seen an accident?'

He shook his head and gave a short, rather hysterical giggle. 'No, a ghost more likely.'

He had the attention of all of them now. 'What's he talking about?' they asked excitedly. 'Where, what happened?'

He looked round. Ellen still looked worried for his sake, his mother still bent over him, Pauline and Tess were staring at him with their mouths open.

'I've been up on the top of the hill, at the Dell.'

'What Dell?'

He shook his head, as if denying what he had just said. 'No, it's a mistake. I didn't see anything.'

'Oh, come on, Tim. You must have seen something to look so queer. What was it?'

He shook his head again and set his lips firmly in a tight line. He could not tell them. The meeting with Percy could not be put into easy words. Perhaps if his mother had been on her own he could have explained, or perhaps he could have told Ellen. But the others, who had teased him all his life, scoffed at everything he did, they could not be trusted with this story. He knew just what they would say, and how they would laugh.

He huddled down in the chair and closed his eyes.

There was a long drawn out rumbling that drew their attention away from him. They looked up at the darkening window.

'Storm's coming,' his mother said, going to the door. 'Tess, come and help me in with the washing.'

The storm certainly was coming. The sky was a dull, leaden grey pressing close to the earth, and a sudden flurry of wind caught at the trees. Pauline switched on the lights and then dashed upstairs to close the windows against the rain.

Ellen looked at him in a questioning sort of way, but she also said nothing. He gave her a wobbly grin, and escaped to his room.

From his window, he watched the storm. Time passed, but no one came to disturb him. He must have stood there, motionless, for an hour. Then, with the coming of night, the lightning and thunder passed a long way away,

25

and there was just an occasional twitch of lightning, and soon he could see and hear nothing at all.

A figure quietly entered the room and Tim, whose nerves were in such a torn state, gave a jump and a gasp of fright. But it was only Ellen, looking strange in the dim half-light.

'It's me.'

They stood companionably together at the window, and Ellen brushed her long, black hair. Tim listened to the quiet noise she made: swish, swish.

'I did see something,' he said.

'I thought so.'

'It's just that I couldn't say in front of the others.'

Ellen nodded. He just managed to see it in the nearly-dark room.

'There was this boy, about my age, up on the hill. He looked very strange. You could tell he was from the future.'

Ellen drew in her breath. 'How?'

'It went very cold, and then he just appeared. I was scared, but he was too.'

'Did he speak?'

'Oh, yes. We talked for a long time. I know you won't believe me.'

Ellen's brush was now still.

'Go on,' was all she could say.

'I can hardly believe it myself, now. At first I was so scared, I thought he was a lunatic. Then we talked and we got to be friends. I don't know how it happened exactly. At least I do, but it's hard to put into words. He was wearing microcybs and they went wrong, so it was all an accident really.'

Ellen held his hand tight.

'Did he do anything?'

'Do anything? No, we just talked. I told you, we just told each other about everything, and got to be friends.'

There was a strange note in Tim's voice that Ellen did not like or understand. She could feel him trembling when she touched him.

'Do you mind if I call Mum?' she asked, her own voice not very steady either.

'No, you can get her now. I don't mind talking about it.'

'And do you mind if I turn on the light?'

'OK.'

She hurried downstairs. Tim slowly got into his pyjamas and waited for them to come. Whatever they made of it, just telling the story would be a relief. The only trouble was, the whole thing sounded less likely and more incredible every time he thought about it.

His mother came in and sat on the bed, Ellen beside her. Obviously she had heard something of what had happened already, because her normally pink face was very pale, and she looked at her son with great concern.

'Now, you just tell me exactly what happened.'

He tried to look and sound normal. 'I saw a sort of apparition. I mean, he wasn't a ghost and he looked real enough, but he told me he was from the future.'

'Ellen said you talked. What did he tell you, what did he say?'

'It was mostly about how life was then, and he wanted to know about mine. He said he lived 500 years from now. He was wearing sort of computers on his head, and one of them was for making us telepathic. It was something going wrong with the computers that sent him back in time.'

He stopped. There was no way of knowing how his mother would take such a story.

'It was someone pulling your leg.'

'No.' The one word hung in the air between them, full of conviction.

Mrs Dunwoodie shook her head in a helpless sort of way. 'I don't say it's impossible. I mean, I do believe in telepathy. I think it runs in the family too. I've had twinges myself, but this is . . .'

Ellen put in gently, 'Tim couldn't have made up such a story could he, Mum? And we don't know what inventions they will have in the future. And this boy *said* it was an accident.'

Tim listened to them, pulling and twisting at a corner of his blanket. 'But Mum, that isn't all he told me. He told me a dreadful thing, something that is going to happen. He said the sea was poisoned in his time, and it was spreading, and all the fish were being killed.'

'Good God, did he say what it was?'

'They didn't know. It seems it comes from something dumped in the sea. And their scientists are all working on it, to try and stop it, and some of them think it has taken hundreds of years to happen.'

'We *are* poisoning it already, so your father says,' Mrs Dunwoodie said sharply. 'All this atomic waste, and oil and I don't know what else.'

Tim shook his head. 'No, it's none of *them*. It must be something else, something that doesn't seem likely to poison anything. Percy said it was a completely new kind of poison.'

'Percy?'

'That was his name.'

Ellen giggled. 'Poor chap, fancy being called Percy.'

Mrs Dunwoodie sat thinking it all over. Tim felt wonderfully comforted to see she actually believed the story. Everything seemed more normal, and gradually he stopped trembling.

'I wish your dad was here.'

'So do I.'

'I don't think it's a story to throw around, though.'

Tim agreed with her. 'Please don't tell the others, Mum,' he begged.

'The only people who ought to know are the scientists. Or someone in the know. They might be able to work it all out and make more sense of it than I can.'

'But who could I tell? We don't know any scientists.'

Tim thought about it, and wondered what a scientist would say. Would he try and help solve the riddle of the poison, or would he laugh and tell him not to be so silly?

'Perhaps Grandad can help,' Ellen said.

'Yes, now that *is* a good idea,' Mrs Dunwoodie agreed. 'He worked at those laboratories at Shenton for years as caretaker. He must have got to know a few scientists.'

'Even if they *do* laugh at me, I'm going to try and save Beppo.'

Ellen creased her forehead. 'Beppo? You said his name was Percy.'

'No, Percy's the boy. Beppo is his dolphin.'

'Dolphin? You didn't say anything about dolphins.'

And so, of course, Tim had to tell them the whole story again, this time leaving out nothing, and before it was finished the church clock struck eleven times. Then Ellen went downstairs to make some cocoa, but before she returned, Tim had fallen asleep on his bed, utterly exhausted. She tucked him in, turned out the light, and gently shut the door.

6

Grandfather

When Tim woke up the next morning, he could feel it was late. He heard the milkman's van driving up the street, clattering the milk bottles; and remembrance of what had happened the day before suddenly flooded in on him. He lay still, thinking and thinking about it, trying to sort out in his mind what had been said, what had been felt, and the tremendous responsibility of it all.

'How can I save Beppo?' he thought, almost with terror. 'Why should this happen to me?'

The answer to that, he knew, was not important. It *had* happened, and out of all the millions of people in England, he was the one involved. It was a very lonely feeling.

Perhaps because he had so much on his mind, or perhaps because he had gone to bed much too late, Tim found himself snapping at everyone and being so unreasonable, that he was soon left alone by the rest of the family.

In the afternoon, his mother said, 'You're like a bear with a sore head. If you can't control your temper you'd better go out. Here, take these clean clothes over to your grandfather's for me. And try and stop *scowling*.'

He said he was too tired, and it was too wet, but in the

end he wheeled his bicycle out of the shed and pedalled the mile to his grandfather's cottage. It was a sodden day; the gutters were gurgling, and wet leaves whirled up in the cold wind.

Grandfather was in. He did not look very pleased to see Tim, perhaps because he had been asleep. But his temper improved when he found half an ounce of tobacco tucked into one of his clean socks.

He put the kettle on, and got down two mugs and the biscuit tin from the kitchen dresser. Tim took a custard cream. Grandfather spooned sugar into their cups and stirred the tea. Then he put his false teeth in and took two biscuits.

'What's the matter with you this afternoon—cat got your tongue?'

'There's nothing wrong with me,' Tim snapped back.

Grandfather snorted. 'Glad to come over here and escape all those sisters?'

There was a not very good-natured silence for a minute or two, and then Tim said, 'You know that place up on the hill, where the plane crashed in the war?'

'You know I know. It was me told you about it.'

'I went there yesterday.'

The old man just looked at him. There was another silence.

'All right. So you went there. What am I supposed to say?'

Tim decided his Grandfather could be a nasty, old, bad tempered man at times. He waited until his pipe was drawing nicely, then tried again.

'I saw someone there.'

This time his grandfather did not even bother to reply.

'He—this person I saw—said he was from the future.'

31

'And I'm the Queen of Sheba.'

Tim stood up. 'If you're going to be like that, I just won't bother to tell you.'

Something in the boy's strained, white face stopped Grandfather from snapping back.

'Sit down, for goodness sake. No need to get so shirty.'

'Will you listen to me, then?'

'Talk some sense, and I'll listen.'

Satisfied, Tim sat down again.

'Don't ask me how it happened, but this boy . . .'

'Boy?'

'Yes, boy about my age—he just appeared from no-where and he looked funny and different and at first I thought he was an escaped lunatic. You know, from the hospital up the way.'

'Well, was he? What made him look funny?'

'I don't mean *funny*. But he was wearing things on his head, wiry things with knobs that looked like blue glass. He said they were little computers.'

'Well. I've heard of some leg pulls in my time . . .'

'It wasn't!' Tim almost shouted. 'I would have known if it was! He got into telepathic communication with me, because they can do that sort of thing, in the future.'

For the first time, Grandfather looked as though he might believe the story. 'Well, that runs in the family, telepathy. Did I ever tell you about the time . . .'

Tim interrupted, 'That's what Mum said.'

'Ah, you've told her, then?'

Tim nodded. 'She doesn't know what to make of it.'

'I'm not surprised. Her son goes off for a walk and comes back and says he's been in touch with the future and talked to some bloke with knobs on.'

'I didn't say she didn't believe me! She does. But she says I ought to see a scientist or someone who knows more about things. Because this boy, he was called Percy, told me something awful that might start happening in our time and poison the sea.'

The old man was sitting up straight in his chair now, his cup of tea growing cold. It was impossible to watch Tim's sincere and desperate face without believing that something had happened to the boy. Even if it turned out to be a hoax, or a dream, he had to take it seriously for Tim's sake.

'I know a few scientists,' he said. 'Don't know if they'll

33

be any help, but when I worked at Grand Universal, I got quite chummy with one or two of 'em. What's all this about poisoning the sea?'

So Tim told the whole story to his Grandfather. At the end of it, he was crying from nerves. Grandfather quietly handed him a handkerchief and tactfully went away to make some more tea.

'You all right now?' he asked when he came back.

'Yes, thanks,' Tim sniffed.

'Well, that's the rummest story I've ever heard. I don't say I don't believe it. I know you couldn't have made it up if you tried, but it takes a bit of swallowing, all the same.'

'Do you think anyone will believe me?'

'Anyone? Well, your Mum does for a start, and Ellen, you say, and I suppose I do too. That's a start, isn't it? We'll do what we can. I'll see if this man I know at Grand Universal will help.'

'Tell a stranger? I can't! He'll laugh!'

'He may, he may not. But you've got to start somewhere, that's if you mean it when you say you'll do anything to save that Beppo.'

'But you won't make it into a joke, will you, Grandad? You won't make fun of it?'

'Tell him yourself, if you think I'm too much of a fool to do it,' the old man replied gruffly.

'I didn't say you were a fool, you know I don't think that. It's just so important that people don't laugh.'

'Well, we don't know he'll even see us yet. And we won't say too much—just enough to give him a few facts to go on. Ask about poisons in the sea and such like.'

'Will he know about chemicals in the sea?'

34

'Sure to. Now, you get off home, and thank your Mum for the tobacco.'

He went, and all the way home, Tim rehearsed in his mind what he would say to the strange scientist. It was no use—the story seemed much to fantastic to convince a stranger and a scientist. Didn't they always like proof?

But his Grandfather's offer to help had cheered him up nevertheless, and he no longer felt he carried all the weight of it on his own. When he got home, his mother was pleased to see him smiling and calm once again.

7

Grand Universal Laboratories

There was not much industry in that part of Kent, and Grand Universal Laboratories was the biggest employer of local men and women in the district. Of course, Grand Universal had factories all over England, but the one at Shenton employed scientists working on research into plastics and food. The number of things the laboratories were involved in meant that some work done there was top secret.

The scientist Grandfather was going to meet shared one thing with the older man: a passion for fishing. They had first met on one of the quiet backwaters in the area, and competed with each other to get the best fish. After that, they would often meet both at work and on the river banks, and talk about the state of the rivers, and where the best fish were to be found; but all Grandfather knew about him was that his name was Crossfield and he was the head of one of Grand Universal's synthesizing departments.

'Dunwoodie? I wonder what he wants with me?' Crossfield frowned when his secretary told him who was on the phone. Then his bushy, sandy eyebrows shot up in surprise when he heard the old man wanted to come and see him, and bring his grandson. He wondered if the boy was interested in becoming a scientist, but he seemed a bit young to be deciding that.

'Could you both be here about 4.30 then?' he asked, looking at his diary. 'I'll meet you downstairs if you ask for me.'

Grandfather then telephoned Tim. 'Wear a clean shirt whatever you do,' he ordered, 'and meet me in time for the ten-to-four bus.'

'Why? Where are we going?'

'Grand Universal, of course,' said Grandfather, very importantly, and hung up.

Tim was very nervous. He cleaned his shoes and borrowed one of his father's nice, big handkerchiefs. His mother tied his tie, and gave him a vague kiss when it was time to go. 'Can't see it will do any harm, talking to this man. But don't expect too much from him, love.'

'But it was you who suggested it!'

'Did I?'

It was obvious she had too many other things on her mind, and Tim felt let down. If the story about Percy did not even interest his own mother, how could he expect it to interest Mr Crossfield? He decided there and then that it would be best only to tell him parts of the story, if he told him anything at all, that was.

Walking down the hill to the bus stop, Tim suddenly panicked. Again he thought, 'Why *me*? Why should I get mixed up in this? Why not just forget all about it?' But he knew he could not. He would never be able to forget the way Percy had looked when he told him about the poisoned sea and about Beppo. Then because he was thinking so hard about Beppo he walked straight into a tree.

'Ouch!' He had hurt his knee, and he bent to rub it.

37

A strange dizziness came over him, and there was a buzzing in his ears. From far off, or near—he could not tell from where—he heard a voice, calling his name.

'Tim! Tim!' it whispered (shouted?).

He looked all around him, but there was no one there. A cold wind stirred the trees and a wet leaf fell on his face. It made him jump.

'Tim!' the voice called again, and suddenly he was sure it was the voice of Percy.

'Percy!' he shouted wildly. 'Where are you?'

Then he heard the voice again, this time quite clearly, saying a name he did not know. 'Tim! It's Tribaxin . . . TRIBAXIN. Can you hear?'

'Yes; yes! Where are you? PERCY!'

But all was still. The dizzy feeling cleared from his head, and he strained his ears for some new sound. But none came.

With a last look about him, he turned and ran down the hill to the bus stop. The strange word kept ringing in his head: Tribaxin. What did it mean?

Grandfather was already at the bus stop. Tim rushed up and started to tell him what had happened, but the old man cut him short.

'Pull your tie straight, you look a scarecrow! And what have you done to your knee?'

He himself was wearing his best, blue suit, and his white moustache was newly trimmed. He looked very nice and very excited.

Tim's attention wandered to something else. He sniffed and then held his nose. 'Hey, what's that awful smell?'

There was a bundle of newspaper under Grandfather's arm from where the smell seemed to emanate.

'If you must know, it's a fish for Mr Crossfield.'

'A *fish*?'

'Yes. A trout I caught up near Paddock.' He was chuckling to himself. 'He'll be green with envy when he sees it.'

'Smells as if the fish is green, more like.'

He got a friendly cuff on the ear for that, and then the bus came, so he did not have a chance to tell Grandfather about the strange voice and the word that had been whispered so urgently.

They sat down in the front of the bus at the top, and then Tim started to feel nervous all over again. His stomach hurt and he wanted to go back home.

'Is he nice?'

'What, Mr Crossfield? Seems decent enough. Goes fishing with me now and then. Not much good, though.' He started to chuckle again and squeezed his fishy bundle tighter. Tim said nothing. He guessed that Mr Crossfield was a very good angler indeed, and that was why Grandfather was going to so much trouble to impress him.

'Ah, here we are. This is where we get off.'

Grand Universal Laboratories was set back from the main road and had a floral clock in front of it. There was also a large car park, and Tim stopped to look at some of the cars.

'Look at that Italian sports! Does it belong to one of the scientists?'

'Must do. Very rich, some of 'em.'

Grandfather was pulling him on towards the front door, very confident and brisk, now he was back in his familiar work ground again. The entrance hall was bright with flowers, and very large. There were black, leather armchairs scattered about. Behind a glass desk sat a receptionist, who welcomed them with a lovely smile. Tim thought she looked like a film star, she had such blonde hair and sparkling jewellery. Her nails were bright red, and the longest he had ever seen.

'Mr Dunwoodie? It *is* nice to see you again.'

She fluttered her eyelashes, and Grandfather took off his hat and fingered his moustache.

'You're looking lovelier than ever, Miss Evelyn. I've come to see Mr Crossfield—I think he expects me.'

They sank down into two armchairs while the lovely Miss Evelyn talked into the telephone on her desk. Tim looked about. He could see nothing that looked like a laboratory. He had expected a sort of hospital smell, and people in white coats everywhere. All he could see, when-ever a door opened off the entrance hall, was what looked like offices, where girls sat typing busily.

The receptionist flashed her smile. 'You're to go down

to the canteen. Mr Crossfield will meet you at the lift.'

They walked down a flight of steps, and a man with sandy eyebrows was waiting for them.

'Mr Crossfield.'

'Mr Dunwoodie.'

They all shook hands, and Tim was introduced.

'Would you like some tea? It's easier to have a chat in the canteen. I've got a lot on upstairs today; there's a bit of a crisis, and we might have been interrupted.'

'I know how busy you are. What we've got to say won't take too long.'

'I didn't mean to hurry you . . .' Mr Crossfield crinkled up his eyes when he smiled, and Tim suddenly decided he liked him. He was not sure how old he was, but he looked younger than his own father. About thirty, he guessed.

They went along the counter with their trays, and Mr Crossfield piled cakes on a plate. 'Come on, take one of those doughnuts. How about some biscuits? Don't be shy. Take two. Orange to drink? Or tea?'

Tim was too shy to say anything, but soon sat down with a large plate of food in front of him.

Grandfather cleared his throat and looked at Mr Crossfield intently. 'Now for it,' Tim thought. 'He's going to tell him now.'

But he did not. 'Have a look in this parcel,' he said, 'I think it might interest you.'

Mr Crossfield unwrapped the newspaper to reveal a large, silvery trout. His eyebrows shot up in surprise.

'What a whopper! Where did you land it?'

Grandfather looked triumphant. 'You know that little stretch past Paddock? Where you said there weren't any trout to be had?'

Mr Crossfield looked disbelieving. 'Never.'

'True as I sit here.'

They all looked at the fish again. It really was beginning to smell strong. Mr Crossfield wrapped it up in the newspaper again and pushed it back to Grandfather.

'No, no, I don't want it back. I meant it for you, it's a little present.'

'That *is* kind.' Mr Crossfield smiled, but Tim noticed he pushed the parcel as far away up the table as he could.

'Is that what you came to see me about?'

Now was the moment. Tim waited, crossing his fingers under the table.

'No. My grandson here would like some advice, and I couldn't think of a better person to come to.'

'Only too glad to help, if I can.'

'It's in your line, I think.'

'My line?' Mr Crossfield scratched his sandy hair, and looked at Tim. 'Do you mean food synthesis?'

'I don't know what that is, sir.' He chose his words with care. 'What I wanted to find out about was to do with poisons. Things that could poison the sea.'

'Ah. You've come to the right man, then. Not so much because of my work, but because of my hobby.'

'You mean fishing?'

'Right. There's nothing I'd like better than to see the rivers pure again, and see some more fish in them.'

'Then you would know what kinds of things poison the sea?'

'All of it? That's a lot of water. I can think of lots of things that might do a bit of local poisoning, but not the *whole* sea.'

'Could you give me a list? Things like oil and detergents?'

'Is this for some kind of school test?'

Tim did not answer but Grandfather cut in. 'He's doing a sort of project. Here you are, here's a bit of paper.'

He produced an old, torn envelope and a stubby pencil. 'Here, write your list on there.'

Mr Crossfield smiled. 'Hold on a minute. It's not that simple, you know. Give me time to think. It doesn't have to be a poison to start with—it's a question of the balance of nature. All sorts of things can act like a poison, put in the wrong place.'

But he wrote some words down all the same, and passed the paper to Tim. 'It's a short list, but I don't think I've left anything out. There's atomic waste and detergent foam, and oil, of course. And sewage.'

Tim thanked him.

'I'm afraid the list will get longer with time. There are so many things dumped in the sea, and some of them are bound to turn out poisonous in the long run.'

There was one thing more Tim wanted to know.

'Please, Sir, have you heard of Tribaxin?'

Mr Crossfield's eyebrows wobbled again. 'Tribaxin! How did you hear about that?'

'I don't know,' Tim floundered.

'It's very new—very hush-hush.' The scientist looked a bit cross that Tim had heard of it.

'Do you mind telling me what we're all talking about?' Grandfather demanded.

Mr Crossfield looked over his shoulder, and then leaned forward so that he could speak in a low voice.

'It's a brand new plastic. Hardly in production yet, and made by some of our boys. When it does come on the market, it's likely to put all the others out of business.

43

Marvellous stuff, so they say.'

'What makes it so special?'

'Ah, that's the secret bit. It has a different structure, different melting point, the lot. You can make anything out of it.'

Tim was dying to know more. His heart was pounding with excitement at this new discovery. So the word did mean something! The voice had been a warning, telling him to do something about Tribaxin, of that he felt sure.

Grandfather was looking at him curiously. 'You never told me about this whatsit. Where did you hear about it?'

'I must have heard someone talking about it on the bus or somewhere.'

The two men seemed satisfied with this explanation. 'Have I helped your project?'

'Oh, yes. Thanks a lot.'

They all stood up. 'And thanks for the lovely tea.'

Mr Crossfield picked up his fish. 'Does your grandson do any fishing?'

'He drops a hook in the water now and then.'

'Perhaps we'll meet up one day, then,' he said, 'and perhaps we'll find this trout's brother.'

The three of them left the building, past the lovely receptionist, who waved good-bye.

'Come again, if you want to,' Mr Crossfield said to Tim.

'Thanks. I will,' he promised.

Back home again, Tim pulled the list out of his pocket and studied it. Somehow, he did not believe the things on the list had anything to do with the poisoned sea. Not any more. Everything on it was so obvious—the scientists in Percy's time would have thought of them all. So it was

44

more likely to be something different, something that nobody would think of. Something like plastic.

He lay on his bed, thinking. Knowing about this Tribaxin was one thing. Knowing what to do next was a bit more difficult.

8

The Wedding

It was time for Tim to go back to school. There was so much to think about that he pushed the problems of Percy, Beppo and Tribaxin to the back of his mind.

It was Ellen who brought the matter up again one day, when the two of them were in the garden picking up windfall apples.

'That boy, Percy, I suppose he knew a terrific lot.'

'Mmm.' Tim answered through the apple he was chewing. 'He did, although there were lots of things he wouldn't tell me. But I suppose there would be more to *know* in 500 years time, anyway.'

'How do you mean?'

'Take us. We know more than they did even a hundred years ago, when there weren't any cars, or aeroplanes or television. Think of all the inventions there must have been between our time and Percy's.'

Ellen thought about it. 'And yet he didn't sound *so* different from us, did he? I mean, in a way, that's a bit of a comfort. In some of these science fiction stories, they make it sound like human beings are going to be monsters, or robots, in the future.'

'There's one thing he did say that might explain why he wasn't all that different. He said he lived in the Age of Simplification. He made it sound like there had been lots of different ages between then and now, and things had gone a bit wild, so they were trying to keep things more normal.'

'I don't understand exactly how you talked to each other, do you?'

'There's lots of it I can't understand. It just happened.'

'I do know it's changed you, though.'

Tim blushed. 'How do you mean?'

'You're much more grown-up because of it. It's really made a difference.'

'I feel the same as always,' he said, going indoors with the basket.

Ellen followed him in. 'What are you doing to do now?'

'I promised Mum to write to Aunt Dorothy and tell her how to get here for the wedding.'

Ellen groaned. 'I'd almost forgotten! What a fuss just over a silly old wedding. I'm going to go off and get married in a registry office—that's *if* I get married.'

'You won't get so many presents,' Tim said practically.

'Who cares? Most of the ones Viv is getting are awful, anyway.'

Preparations for the wedding had been going on for so long, it seemed that chaos was the normal state of affairs in the Dunwoodie household. There were always packets and parcels lying about on the chairs, and sewing everywhere. Van after van kept arriving with food and drink, and Mrs Dunwoodie was up at dawn every day, she had so much to do. There was the village hall to be booked, the cars to be hired, the photographer told to be there, the banns to be read, and the invitations to be sent out. Mr Dunwoodie arrived home from a business trip in time to order some more drinks, buy a new pair of shoes, get his hair cut, and try to prepare his speech. Tim very wisely stayed out of his father's way during this trying time, and nothing was said to Mr Dunwoodie about the business of Percy and the future poisoned sea.

Tim was given a new suit that he secretly thought was marvellous. He went round to show it to Grandfather, and found him very busy too. He was making a small, inlaid workbox for the bride's wedding present, and it was a pleasure to watch as he lovingly polished each fine piece of rosewood and ebony, and fitted them together.

'Not that I'll be there,' he declared. 'Can't stand crowds of relations, all saying nasty things about each other behind their backs.'

'But you've got to be there,' Tim insisted. 'You're the head of the family.'

Grandfather looked pleased about that. 'Well, I'll see how my arthritis is. If it's playing up, I won't go.'

In fact, he did. And so did Uncles Harold, Arthur, and Will, and Aunts Violet, Dorothy, Emma and Jane, with all their children and grandchildren too. And all the bridegroom's family was there, and all the friends of the two families. Almost half the village packed the church. Tim and his mother sat in the front of the pews on one side, and the bridegroom's mother and father sat on the other side of the church. Tim found there were all sorts of rules about weddings. The bridegroom had to stand and wait at the altar with someone called the best man, and then the organ played a beautiful tune and the bride came up the aisle on the arm of her father, followed by Tess, Pauline and Ellen in their bridesmaids' dresses. He hardly recognized any of them, especially the bride: they looked so beautiful.

After the service, photographs were taken on the church steps, and Tim pulled a face in the ones that included him. Then they were taken by cars to the village hall, although it was only a few hundred yards away.

Tim forgot about rules and enjoyed himself. They ate chicken and ham salad and trifles and jellies, and drank white wine. Then he was given a glass of champagne with a tiny piece of the wedding cake.

'Don't drink it yet, you daft thing!' Ellen hissed. 'You have to wait for the toast.'

He looked around, but could not see any toast. Then he was glad he hadn't said anything, because he found out that 'toast' meant a lot of boring speeches by the bridegroom, his father, and the best man. Then Grandfather got up to say a few words, and then Uncle Will. And only then was he free to leave the table and chase his cousins round the hall. They found quite a lot of glasses with drink still in, and Uncle Arthur gave him a glass of beer.

Mrs Dunwoodie stood near the door, smiling at everybody, feeling sad and happy at the same time. It really had been worth all the effort, she thought; a really wonderful wedding it had been. No one had been rude to Aunt Jane, who could be very touchy at times, and Uncle Will had not drunk too much. Vivien came up to hug her mother, before dashing back to their house to change into her travelling clothes. (They were going to Majorca for their honeymoon.)

'Good-bye, my darling. Have a lovely time.'

She couldn't help crying a little bit. There were all the other girls to see to in the future, and by the way Pauline was flirting, the next wedding wouldn't be too far ahead, she decided. Even young Tim seemed to be having a good time. He had been looking too quiet lately, but perhaps the wedding would help get that other business out of his mind. No sense in troubling Dad with the story now, he had enough on his mind with the worry and expense of the wedding. The whole thing would blow over, she was sure, and Tim would settle down and be his old self again.

Back home, later that night, Ellen sadly took off her pale blue dress with the rosebuds round her neck, and carefully hung it up at the back of her wardrobe. Tim stopped to watch her, as he went to get on his pyjamas.

'Did you enjoy it, El?'

'It was lovely. Did you?'

'Mmm. The food was all right. But what a *performance*!'

Ellen laughed and said, 'Well, your friend Percy would have enjoyed it. That's what he calls social history, isn't it?'

'I suppose he would call it that. Do you think they will do things differently in 500 years from now?'

''Course. They won't be tying old boots on the back of jet-packs or rockets, will they?'

'I didn't ask him about churches. That's something else they might not have. What do you think, El?'

But Ellen would not commit herself one way or the other, and soon they said good-night to each other and each went to bed.

9

The Sea

It was the next fine morning after the wedding and the Dunwoodies were having Sunday breakfast together.

'Dad, what about going to the sea today?' Ellen asked.

Tim looked at her quickly. It was odd, but he had just been about to ask the same thing. He and Ellen seemed to share the same thoughts quite a lot, these days.

Their father put down the newspaper and nodded, but a bit doubtfully. 'It's OK with me. It's up to your mother.'

'I'd planned a cold lunch today anyway, so it won't upset me—as long as you all help me get ready.'

'If we all do something, we can leave in about half an hour,' Ellen said eagerly, 'and beat the traffic.'

'Can Grandfather come too?' Tim asked.

'We don't want to go, do we, Tess?' Pauline said. 'We're going to be busy.' They both giggled, and the rest of the family groaned.

'Out with those boys again! All right, that means there will be plenty of room for Grandad, if he wants to come.'

Tim raced upstairs to make his bed and get his swimming things. He knew the sea would be cold, but it was worth going in, all the same. He put his cricket ball and bat in the duffle bag along with his towel and trunks, and felt excited. It was going to be a lovely Sunday!

They collected Grandfather on the way, and because they reached the sea so early, they had the beach almost to themselves for a while. There was a cold wind, but the sea sparkled and glistened whenever the sun came out, and they kept warm after a quick dip in the big waves by running about, playing French cricket.

At about midday, Grandfather got up stiffly from his deckchair and gave Tim a wink. 'Coming for a little stroll?' he asked.

Tim nodded eagerly. He knew exactly what that meant; it meant they would walk along the front to one of the old pubs, and sit down outside on a bench. Grandfather would have a pint of ale, and he would have a lemonade and some crisps.

They climbed over a breakwater, the old man very stiffly. 'Whoever invented deckchairs couldn't have ever sat in one,' he grumbled. 'I'm glad to stretch my legs.'

'Never mind, Grandad. Aren't you glad you came?'

They looked at the sea, at the birds squealing overhead and at a line of small sailing boats getting ready to start a race.

'Takes a morning like this to make you realize what your friend Percy's had to give up.'

'I'd almost forgotten,' Tim said, guilt flooding him because of it. 'I thought you had, too.'

'Well, so I had, but there was something in the paper this morning reminded me.'

'What?'

'Here. I've got it on me.' He pulled a much-folded newspaper out of his back pocket. 'You read it.' They sat down outside the Rose and Crown. 'I can't see without my glasses.'

'But you're wearing them!'

'Not these glasses. These are my wearing glasses. I mean my reading glasses.'

Tim shrugged and started to read the article Grandfather pointed to.

'Dr Paul Mackenzie, zoologist of Oxford University, claims that dolphins dance. In an article in the current issue of *Nature*, Dr Mackenzie reports on the habits of the Mediterranean dolphin, which he studied for five months last year off the Greek coast. He describes their behaviour and social habits, and suggests that, at certain times, their swimming movements fall into curious patterns.

'It is like some sort of ritual dance,' he writes. 'I have seen several individuals in a school repeat these movements over and over again. The action seems unrelated to courtship ceremonies, nor does it seem to constitute part of their "games". It is as if the animals were performing a dance-drama in front of their companions.'

'Gosh,' said Tim. 'Like Percy said it would be! I wonder if this Doctor is the man he meant, when he said someone found out about the dance four hundred years ago. Perhaps he had got his dates a bit wrong, and it is starting now.'

Grandfather disappeared to get their drinks and two packets of crisps.

They sat looking out at the green and silver sea.

'It's awful to think it's all going to change,' Tim said sadly.

'Don't worry. We'll beat it yet,' Grandfather said firmly.

'Are you going to help me again, then?'

'I'm all for a bit of a fight. You know me.'

'But what can we do?'

'We can go back to your mum and get some food. That's what we can do. I'm starving, aren't you? Just leave the thinking to me.'

They did not speak about Percy and the dolphins any more. It was just an ordinary, late autumn day by the sea. At the back of Tim's mind, helping him to appreciate the simple things they did, was the thought that one day all this would be poisoned. It made it all seem more special.

The next night, Tim sat biting his fingernails, trying to do his homework.

'El, what was the Thirty Years War all about?'

Ellen pretended not to hear.

'ELLEN.'

'Oh, leave me alone, can't you? I've got my own work to do. *And* it's harder than yours. If you don't know, you'll just have to tell your teacher you can't do it.'

'Oh, yes, very funny,' he jeered. 'Just like you, I suppose, when you couldn't do your geometry and cried all over the place.'

'Mum, tell him to shut up!'

'Stop it, you two,' she said calmly, going on with darning one of Tim's jerseys. 'Your father went to a lot of expense, buying that set of encyclopaedias. I can't think why he bothered—none of you ever look anything up in them.'

Tim went over to the bookshelves.

'What shall I look under? Thirty?'

Ellen raised her eyes to the ceiling. 'No. Try looking it up under twelve and three-quarters.'

He pretended not to hear this sarcastic remark.

'Thargelia . . . what on earth is that? Here we are—

54

Thirty Years War.' He read for a few moments, then started to flip the pages again. 'Hey, these books aren't bad. There's pages and pages about the theatre. Drawings and everything. And there's thermodynamics . . .'

When their homework was finished, it was time for bed. Tim took down a different volume of the encyclopaedia, chose the juiciest looking apple in the fruit bowl, and kissed his mother good-night.

'What's that you've got?'

'An apple.'

'No, silly! I mean the book.'

'It's a bit of the encyclopedia.'

His mother looked pleased. 'You're getting to be a clever boy. That school seems to suit you.'

'It's all right.'

'Well, don't read too long.'

Up in his tiny room, he quickly got ready for bed, and then drew the heavy book on his knee. It must have weighed pounds.

'What a weight. Lucky old Percy keeps all *his* books on his head!' he thought, opening the encyclopaedia at the page he wanted. There it was . . .

'*Dolphinus delphis* . . . black above, white below . . . about six feet long . . . makes noises, both as a language and supersonically . . . has between 160 and 200 teeth . . . follows ships . . .'

Not much there, really. Tim bit into his apple and thought about Beppo. Percy had said they had not met any other form of life from outer space. It was funny to think how much time and energy people spent rushing off to planets and the moon, trying to discover things, when all the time, right here under the sea, waiting for the right questions to be asked, was a creature

55

of tremendous intelligence and fun: the dolphin.

He felt very wise. He knew more about dolphins than even the encyclopaedia.

He threw his apple core out of the window, and curled up ready for sleep. The book slid off the bed and fell on the floor with a heavy thump.

The Competition

It was just before the biology lesson, and the master took Tim on one side.

'That was a nice bit of work you handed in, Dunwoodie.'

'Thank you, sir.'

'Are you keen on science?'

'I think so, sir.'

'Good. I expect it's all a bit new yet, but you show promise.'

Tim felt shy and yet pleased to be singled out for such praise.

'I've got something to tell you all,' said the master, raising his voice, 'so settle down. Let's have some quiet.'

When the class were all giving him at least part of their attention, he held up a magazine for them to see.

'I don't know if any of you have ever seen this. It's a monthly magazine called *Scientific Knowledge*. Anyone read it?'

One or two boys put up their hands hesitatingly.

'Good. Then you'll know it's aimed at making science popular and easy for the man in the street to understand. They think it might even interest a few boys in the street.'

They groaned.

'Well, now. This month the magazine is setting a competition for boys and girls under sixteen, and I thought you might like to have a bash at it.'

'What sort of prizes are they giving, sir?'

'First prize is ten pounds. . . .'

They whistled and laughed.

'Tell us how to get rich!'

'It's worth having a go, then.'

'Be quiet, and let me finish. The subject they have set is, "Living in a Computer Age".'

There were more groans.

'All right. I know it's difficult. But if any of you want the details, come and see me after the lesson.'

Tim was one of the boys who copied the details into their exercise books. He knew exactly what he was going to write. Instead of going home after school, he sat in the library and wrote for about half an hour without stopping. At Mrs Nelson's shop in the village, he bought a big envelope and a stamp. There and then, he posted off his entry to the competition: 'Living in a Computer Age—in A.D. 2500.' It caught the six o'clock post.

'I didn't even read it through,' he thought later. 'Oh, well. It won't win, anyway.'

He went out to see if Victor was free to have a game of conkers, and forgot all about it.

Breakfast at the Dunwoodies was always a hurried affair during the week. Mr Dunwoodie was the only one who seemed to have time to have two cups of coffee and read the paper.

'Good Lord!' he exclaimed, holding up the front page.

'What's up, Dad?' Tim asked, through his cornflakes.

58

'Listen to this. A boat's sunk. "Disaster at Sea. The 5,000 ton merchant vessel, *Honour Bound* is feared to have sunk in mid-Atlantic in the early hours of this morning. At 1 a.m., ships in the vicinity picked up a distress signal. Two of them reported seeing flames reaching up for hundreds of feet in the sky, and rushed to the *Honour Bound*'s aid. By 3 a.m., she was reported to be listing heavily, but all crew members, including the captain, were taken on board the *Sister Elsie* before the ship slowly disappeared, still ablaze from stem to stern, in the first light of dawn."'

He looked up. 'Seems funny, a fire at sea. You'd think with all that water about, it wouldn't have a chance to catch hold.'

'Was it an old ship?' Tim asked, not terribly interested, but wanting to be polite.

His father went on reading. 'No, she wasn't. It says she only went into service fifteen months ago. Here, you'd better read it yourself. I'll be late.'

He threw Tim the paper, and grabbed hold of Ellen to give her a kiss, as she came flying into the kitchen, late for breakfast.

'When will you be back, Daddy?' she asked, grabbing him round the waist and going with him to the front door.

'Friday. Be a good girl.' He rumpled her hair and gave her another kiss, then Ellen shut the front door after him and went back to the kitchen, humming a little tune.

She stopped when she saw Tim's face.

'Hey, what's the matter? You look terrible!'

He seemed not to hear. He picked up the paper, which had somehow got dropped in the milk, and disappeared upstairs to his room. There, he sat down on his bed, and read again the words that had made him turn so pale.

'The ship's owners say her cargo was a mixed one. Apart from several cases of Irish whiskey and some farm machinery, the s.s. *Honour Bound* was carrying the first consignment of household goods made in this country from a new wonder plastic: Tribaxin.'

Tribaxin. And the *Honour Bound* had sunk in mid-Atlantic. And Percy had said that the poisoning had started from the mid-Atlantic.

'It's just got to fit,' he said, seeing his sister standing at the door.

'What's got to fit? What are you talking about?'

'Oh, it's so difficult to explain. It's about this boat that sunk last night. It had Tribaxin on board, and Percy said the word Tribaxin to me. I'm sure it was a warning.'

'I don't understand a word you're talking about.'

'Look here. Read it for yourself. Then I'll try and explain.'

A few minutes later, Ellen and Tim sat together, looking very thoughtful.

'Let's have a look at the atlas. Have you got one?'

Ellen fetched her atlas from her satchel. They studied the map of the Atlantic Ocean.

'Look here. If the boat sunk anywhere about *here*, the currents would be right. There's lots of them, do you see, all at different depths. And there's a sort of mountain range down there, the Atlantic Ridge. A boat could easily get stuck down in one of the valleys and not drift about too much. The poison would get carried this way by the currents.'

'But we don't know it was the Tribaxin. We don't even know the boat *did* sink in that part of the sea.'

Tim set his mouth in a thin line of determination, and

when he spoke, it sounded like a vow. 'I don't know *yet*. But I'm going to find out. And I'm going to try and stop any more of this stuff getting thrown about.'

Ellen was impressed. 'Do you think we could start by ringing somebody up and finding out exactly where the boat did sink?'

They thought about it for a moment.

'Listen,' Ellen said at last. 'I'll do it. I'll ring up the owners—it gives their names here—and pretend I'm a reporter on the *Kent Messenger*. Then we'll get some more details to work on.'

'Would you? Could you?' Tim was a little scared.

But Ellen was not. She had really entered into the spirit of the thing by the time she reached the telephone. She asked the operator, in a very grown-up way, to connect her to the Roberts Line in Trafalgar Square. 'Here goes,' she whispered, as they heard the telephonist at the other end answer, 'Roberts Line. Good morning.'

'Oh, hello. I want to speak to your Press Officer, please. He isn't in? Is there anyone else there I can speak to, I'm from the *Kent Messenger*.'

There were a few clicks on the line, and Ellen gave her brother a triumphant wink. Then she spoke again into the mouth piece.

'I'm enquiring about the *Honour Bound*. I want to know if any local men were hurt or lost at sea. Pardon? Oh, that's good. It would help my story if you could tell me exactly where she went down.'

She signalled wildly for a pen, and wrote some figures down on the telephone book cover.

'Thank you. Yes, I've got that. You've been most helpful. Good-bye.'

Tim slapped her on the shoulder with glee. 'It worked!

What did they say, El? You sounded just like a reporter, you were great!'

Ellen leaned against the wall, looking quite shaky now it was over.

'Here, I wrote down the latitude and longitude on the phone book. Now we'll see exactly where it went down.'

They rushed upstairs to look at the atlas again. Tim made a small pencil cross where the longitude and latitude met. They looked at each other.

The *Honour Bound* had sunk just above the deepest part of the mid-Atlantic Ridge, slightly to the west of the high and low currents that flowed towards Europe.

'That proves it. That's good enough for me,' Tim said. 'The poison started from there, the Tribaxin went down there. It must be what Percy meant.'

'You'll have a hard time convincing people it's a poison.'

Somewhere a clock struck the half-hour. Ellen jumped. 'Is that the time? I'll be ever so late for school. Let's leave it until tonight.'

'Crikey! I'll be late as well!' Tim grabbed his satchel and flew downstairs. He had his cycle out of the shed before Ellen had reached the kitchen door.

'See you tonight, then,' he called, wobbling off down the road.

'Yes, 'bye.' Ellen called, struggling into her blazer and hoping the school bus would be as late as it usually was.

On the steep hill down to his school, Tim wheeled the bike into the gutter and stopped. He sat on the saddle, balancing with his toes, and gave himself up to deep thought. Then he came to a decision.

'No. I won't go to school. I can't just go on as if noth-

62

ing had happened. Even if it does mean trouble, I've just got to get this thing sorted out.'

Before he could change his mind, he turned the front wheel round and pedalled as fast as he could back to the crossroads, and took the left fork that led to Shenton. and Grand Universal Laboratories.

II

Grand Universal Again

'If I don't do something, there's no one else will,' Tim muttered to himself, as he chained his bike to the car park railings. He kept saying it. It gave him a little courage.

The beautiful receptionist was at her desk. She gave him a dazzling smile, although he was sure she did not remember him. Her fingernails were now a dull gold.

'Is Mr Crossfield in?'

Her smile wavered for a moment.

'Mr Crossfield is a very busy man, dear.' But she relented. 'All right. I'll see if he's free.'

She dialled a number on her telephone and leaned across to Tim. 'What shall I say?' she whispered.

'Say Tim Dunwoodie wants to see him. Urgently.'

She talked into the telephone, then said, 'Well, it seems he can see you. Take the lift. Third floor, room 305.'

He thanked her and got into the lift. He had never worked one like this before, and he hoped he had got it right. He pushed a button with '3' on it, and the doors whooshed shut and he felt himself rise. He got out and almost ran down the corridor to room 305, not daring to give himself time to turn round and go back to school.

'Come in,' said Mr Crossfield.

He was sitting behind a littered desk. Through a door to the right, Tim caught a glimpse of men in white coats, busily putting together something that looked like an animal cage with a television set inside it. It looked very interesting, but Tim did not have time to investigate.

'Hallo, Tim.' If Mr Crossfield was surprised to see him, he managed to hide it, and his smile was friendly as he told Tim to sit down and make himself comfortable.

'Have you come on your own?' he added, as Tim still could not find anything to say.

'I didn't tell Grandfather I was coming. I had to see someone urgently, someone who could help, and I thought of you.'

'Nothing wrong, I hope? You sound upset.'

'I want to get some help. It's about Tribaxin.'

Mr Crossfield's eyebrows rose an inch. 'Tribaxin? The new plastic? Didn't you mention it before? I don't quite see . . .'

'Please, Mr Crossfield, I don't know who else to go to. I've told the story to Grandfather and my mother, and my sister. But they aren't experts or anything. I thought you might be able to help, because you're a scientist, and perhaps you can stop them making any more.'

Mr Crossfield opened his mouth, but said nothing. He could see that Tim was very distressed, but he had no idea what he was talking about.

After a moment, he said, 'Until you explain, I don't know if I can help or not. Suppose you start at the beginning?'

This is it, Tim thought. The moment he had dreaded, when he would have to tell a stranger all about the meeting with Percy.

'Some time ago, a few weeks back, I went for a walk.

65

Call it a dream, or whatever you like, but I met a boy and he said he was from the future, and he told me they could get in touch with each other telepathically in his time, because they wore sort of computers on their heads. I could see him as clear as I see you, and I could see these knobs on his head, the computers. He said his had suddenly got twisted up and gone wrong, and somehow he had come back into our time, 500 years back.'

'How exciting,' Mr Crossfield broke in. 'It's absolutely enthralling, just like a story in a book. Did you talk to each other or just read each other's minds?'

'Both. That's how I'm sure it was real and not a hoax. I mean, I really felt this telepathy.' Tim stopped in surprise. Mr Crossfield was sitting there, his eyebrows going up and down, and he believed him!

'Go on,' he urged.

'Well, he told me something that was terrible. He said that the sea was poisoned in his time, and no one could work out what it was. It wasn't anything usual, and it worked by what he called a chain reaction, so it got worse and worse. He told me about how the fish were all dying, and the dolphins. He had a pet dolphin, you see, and it hurt him very much to see it dying.'

Mr Crossfield lit a cigarette and started to pace up and down the room. But he was still listening intently.

'Well, anyway, on the day I came to see you with Grandfather, I was sure I heard Percy's voice, sort of calling me and trying to warn me about something. And he said this word, "Tribaxin", over and over again. I'm sure I've never heard the word before, and you said it was brand new, but I didn't somehow think it could have anything much to do with the poisoned sea. I didn't think it was important.'

'It's important all right, but I don't see how it fits into your story.'

'I didn't either, until today. You see, Percy, that's the name of this boy, told me the poisoning started in the middle of the Atlantic, and drifted east. Last night a boat sunk at exactly the right spot, and it was loaded with Tribaxin.'

'You think Tribaxin is the poison? It's just not possible. Plastics can't just turn into poison. At least, they haven't ever done so.'

Mr Crossfield looked quite pale.

'Have you ever heard the word, "benign"? Well, plastic is benign, it isn't malignant, like poison.'

'It wouldn't have turned into a poison overnight. It took years and years. It might have got mixed up with something else in the shipwreck or in the sea. It's got to be Tribaxin. The word came into my head, and I'm sure it was Percy's voice, and then it sinks in just the right bit of the sea like that . . .'

Tim's voice trailed away. It suddenly seemed to him quite an impossible and silly thing. He got up. 'I'd better go.'

'You stay where you are. You're not going until I've had time to think about it for a bit.'

Mr Crossfield opened one of his desk drawers and got out a folder. 'I've got some information on Tribaxin here. What it's made of, how it's made, what you can do with it. Give me a minute, and I'll try and work something out.'

Tim sat and watched him making notes all over a piece of paper. He stopped writing and squinted at Tim.

'One thing, though. The scientists in the future are working on it, you say? So in the time since you spoke to

Percy and now, they may have got it beat.'

'I suppose they could have. They were working on it, Percy said.'

'So whatever we do now, they may not need your help after all.'

'You mean, we may as well not do anything,' Tim said humbly, 'just in case they can stop it themselves?'

'Put like that, it sounds a bit cowardly. But, yes, I suppose that's what I mean. Think, Tim, how much more knowledgeable they will be than we are.'

'But Percy went to a lot of trouble, I'm sure he must have, to get that message to me. He must have had a reason. Why should he have bothered if he thought they could do it themselves?'

Mr Crossfield said nothing for a while, but then seemed to come to a decision. 'All right. Good. We shall assume he needs help, and the responsibility rests with us.'

He looked at his paper again. 'I don't know . . . it might just be possible, if the reaction was over a long time . . . let me see . . .'

He made signs all over the place but seemed to get nowhere.

'Another thing, Tim. If we stop making it at Grand Universal, someone, somewhere else, is bound to discover it sooner or later. That's the way science works. Then what could we do?'

'But if you proved it was dangerous, couldn't the scientists make it differently?'

'I can't say. I haven't worked on it.'

'Who do you have to tell, if you think it is the poison?'

'There's only one man who says yes or no to things like this. That's the Managing Director of Grand Universal.' He smiled grimly. 'And no one tells *him* he's made a mistake—not if he wants to keep his job, that is.'

'Oh.'

'Yes, he's the man to see. Sir Arthur Bernard Mac-Leish.'

Tim stood up. His voice was wobbling a little, but he asked, 'Where can I find him?'

Mr Crossfield stared. 'You mean you're going through with it?'

'I've got to. If I don't, no one else in the world will.'

'He's upstairs on the fifth floor. I mean, that's where he is, if he's here. But he won't see you.'

Tim was already opening the door. 'I've got to try.'

With a sigh, Mr Crossfield got up and joined him.

'Come on, then. Let's get it over.'

'Do you mean you'll come with me?'

'Of course I'll come with you. You can't keep all the fun to yourself!'

The fifth floor had thick, grey carpets on the floor and oil paintings on the walls. Mr Crossfield spoke in a whisper before opening a polished door. 'You leave all the talking to me, do you hear?'

Tim nodded. Having Mr Crossfield help him was so wonderful, he felt almost brave. Inside the office, a calm, stately old lady sat behind a desk, and looked up from some papers when Mr Crossfield and Tim went in.

'Mr Crossfield?'

'Is Sir Arthur in?'

She looked at them steadily. 'I can see no appointment in the diary, Mr Crossfield.'

'There isn't one. I mean, I didn't make one. But I've got to see him today.'

They heard someone in the next room opening a drawer.

'No one, *no one* sees Sir Arthur without an appointment.'

'This time,' Mr Crossfield said firmly, 'they do!'

He took Tim's arm in a steely grip and pushed open the door of the Managing Director's office.

There was a small, very fat man sitting behind the huge desk. He looked so surprised to see them, he opened his mouth wide. Then he closed it abruptly and pulled himself together.

Tim tried to hide behind Mr Crossfield, but covertly examined the Managing Director of Grand Universal Laboratories. He was very pink and shiny, with gold rimmed spectacles and very little hair. Fat bulged over the collar of his grey suit. His eyes were the same colour, light grey, and as cold as stone. His voice, when he spoke finally, was strong and deep, the voice of someone used to giving orders.

'What do you mean by barging in here, Crossfield? And who's *that*?' He pointed with distaste at Tim.

Mr Crossfield cleared his throat. 'Excuse me, Sir Arthur. I had to see you, because something important has come up. I wanted you to hear it straight away.'

'What's the boy doing here?'

'He has something to do with this—this discovery. It's about Tribaxin.'

'Go on.'

'Apparently a boat sank today carrying the first load of Tribaxin to the States . . .'

'You burst in here like a maniac to tell me that! I've had people phoning me since four o'clock this morning!'

'Yes, sir. It's not the actual sinking I wanted to warn

you about, but what the sinking may mean. We have reason to believe the Tribaxin may slowly deteriorate into a poison—it could be very serious.'

'What are you talking about? You haven't even been working on Tribaxin, have you? Where's your proof?'

'I haven't any. Not yet, anyway. If you give me time, I think I've got an idea of what may happen. I want to get working on it right away.'

'Do you now?'

'And in the meantime, if you don't mind, sir, I think it might be wise to stop making any more.'

Sir Arthur was so taken aback, he spluttered when he answered. 'Do you take me for a fool?'

'No sir. Of course not.'

'Well, do you think we haven't tested this stuff? Do you think we don't make sure our products are safe? How dare you tell me my business.' As he paused for breath, Mr Crossfield and Tim instinctively took a few steps back.

'Do you know our record of safety? Our things are better tested, more thoroughly investigated, than anyone's in the world. If some silly fool takes too much of a medicine, he may get a rash, that's all.'

'I'm not talking about a rash, sir. I'm talking about a serious chain reaction that could spread all over the sea.'

'So you tell me. With no proof whatsoever. I think you've taken leave of your senses, Crossfield, I really do. I've just told you, all our products are thoroughly tested.'

'There could be a slip-up. Something no one thought to test.' He was a stubborn man, Mr Crossfield, but Tim knew it was no use.

'You've got a good record here, otherwise I'd think seriously about your position. This is no way for a scientist to act. Give me positive, scientific proof, or else keep out of my way.'

His tone was final. He pressed a buzzer on his desk. 'Miss Falkirk will see you out.'

They left the room in silence. Tim tried to think of something to say to cheer up Mr Crossfield. He had probably ruined his career, and it was Tim's fault. And they had failed.

Mr Crossfield came with him to the front door. 'I'm sorry, Tim,' was all he could say.

'It's all right. It's not your fault. I . . . I think I'd better get off home now.'

'I'll be in touch.' He squeezed Tim's shoulder briefly, and went back to the lift.

Tim got his bicycle and tried hard not to cry. Then he slowly cycled to Grandfather's house. He just could not face either school or home.

12

Letters

The old man was opening a tin of meat pudding when Tim arrived. He did not look terribly pleased to see his grandson.

'No school today?'

'I played truant.'

'Well, don't expect much of a dinner. There's not much in these tins.'

He divided the hot pudding between two plates, and added some mashed potatoes and gravy. 'Want some peas?'

'No. I'm not very hungry.'

But he ate the pudding up all the same, while he told Grandfather all about what had happened that morning.

'Business!' the old man exploded. 'I don't know what happens to people, when they get into business. Just because he's got lots of money wrapped up in this Tribaxin, that man will never change his mind. He won't care if he poisons all the seas between here and China so long as he makes a profit.'

'So, you see, its hopeless.'

' 'Course it's not. Big things don't come easy. Stands to reason you've got to fight harder for big things. Those boys at the top think they know everything, but they

74

don't. We'll give 'em a run for their money.'

He sounded so definite and cheerful that Tim found himself beginning to hope all over again.

'I suppose we could try something else.'

'No suppose about it. That's how things are done—if you can't ginger up one lot, you ginger up the next. Now then, we'll start by writing a letter to all the papers, and to our M.P., and all the scientists we can think of.'

'Will we?'

'We'll have everyone in the country talking about it before we're done. That will show old Sir Arthur what's-his-name!'

One paper printed their letter, and one weekly magazine; seventeen others did not. They had a post card from their M.P., acknowledging their kind letter which would receive his attention. There was no further word from him. Tim was almost in despair.

'Doesn't anyone care?'

'It looks bad, I'll admit. Never mind, we'll have another go at the scientists.'

'What scientists?'

Grandfather was irritable. 'What's the matter with you? Everything I suggest, you just make difficulties! Just *scientists*. Big ones, little ones, whoever we can.'

Grandfather loved a crusade. He looked ten years younger than he had at the beginning of their letter campaign. 'I'll get a list together, and you can make some more copies of the letter.'

Tim was tired of the letter. He and Ellen had written it so many times, it no longer had any meaning. They had tried to type it on their father's old portable typewriter, but that made it twice as messy, and it took longer

75

than writing by the time they had rubbed out their mistakes. So they went back to pen and ink.

They were in Tim's bedroom early in the evening, trying to do as many as possible before they got too cold.

'Let's stop,' Ellen urged. 'It's worse than writing lines. We've done twenty-seven of the beastly things, anyway.'

'OK.' He stretched to get the ache out of his hunched back. 'Thanks for the help.'

'I've been thinking. Do you think it would be better if you went to see someone else—better than writing these letters, I mean? Someone like the Prime Minister.'

'Ellen! I couldn't! Not after Sir Arthur.'

The truth was, Tim no longer felt brave or clever enough to convince anybody. He sighed. 'Sometimes I wish I'd never met Percy, I really do.'

Ellen said nothing, but he knew she understood, which was a comfort.

'I'm not saying I'm giving up. It's just so—oh, you know. It's not my world—it's a grown-up's world, and they can't be bothered to listen.'

'I know. But you've said often enough, if you don't do it, no one will. I think it's marvellous how you've kept on with it. I really do. Come on, it's bed time. Let's leave the rest until tomorrow, and perhaps you'll not feel so down about it then.'

'Good-night, then, El.'

'Good-night, Tim.'

She gathered all the papers together tidily and gave him one of her toffees, just to cheer him up.

His mother woke him up the next morning by calling up the stairs. 'Tim, come on down. There's a letter for you. It looks important.'

76

'Hang on. I'm just coming,' he shouted. He wondered who it could be from. One of the newspapers! But no, it couldn't be, because they had used Grandfather's address on all the letters.

He took the envelope with curiosity. It said 'Scientific Knowledge' in the corner. There was a cheque pinned to a letter inside.

'Dear Timothy,' it said: 'We are pleased to tell you that your entry for the "Living in a Computer Age" competition has been awarded a prize. The judges were very impressed by your imaginative essay, and they have decided to divide first prize between you and another boy. Both essays will appear in our next issue of *Scientific Knowledge*, a copy of which will be sent to you later this month. We have much pleasure in enclosing a cheque for five pounds, your share of the winning ten pounds prize, and take this opportunity to congratulate you on winning.'

'Cor!' was all he could say.

His mother took the letter. 'May I see?' She gasped when she read it. 'Girls! Look here. Tim's won five pounds!'

They all crowded round to see.

'We didn't even know you'd gone in for it. What did your essay say?'

'I can hardly remember it now. It was about people living in the future.' He stared at the cheque, still not believing he had won.

'What will you spend it on?'

'Is that why you've been up in your room, writing such a lot?'

'You *are* a dark horse!'

Tim tried to escape. 'I'd better take the letter to school and show Mr Barnes.'

'He *will* be pleased.'

But Mr Barnes, the science master, knew about it already, because the entry had given the name of Tim's school, and the magazine had sent a letter to him, too.

Tim's winning essay was the subject of the Head's talk after Assembly Prayers that morning, and it was thrilling, and a bit embarrassing, to have his news told to the whole school. Afterwards a crowd of boys came up to congratulate him and ask questions about it.

'When can we read it?'

'In the next issue, I think they said. I didn't make a copy.'

Everyone had advice on what to spend his five pounds on. After a lot of discussion, Tim decided he would buy a camera.

For days afterwards, boys he hardly knew smiled at him, and told him about the different cameras they owned. It was a lovely week.

On the day his free copy of *Scientific Knowledge* arrived, he took it to school, and the essay was pinned on the notice board. He took it down a bit later to show it to Grandfather.

'Ah, you've brought it, then.' Grandfather took something out of his pocket and put it in Tim's hand. It was a crumpled up pound note.

'Before I forget. Take this to add to your winnings. Help get a better camera.'

Tim stammered his thanks. He was very moved—he knew Grandfather only had his old-age pension to live on, and it was the first time the old man had given him a present of money.

'Don't make a fuss about it. You're a good boy, and it's about time I gave you a present.'

'Shall I read the essay, or fetch you your glasses?'

'You read it to me. Just let me settle myself. Right.'

Tim cleared his throat, and began to read.

' "Living in a Computer Age—in A.D. 2500 By Tim Dunwoodie.

' "When we think about computers today, we think of big machines that are very expensive. They are fed with information at one end and give answers on tape or a display board. They are generally found in big businesses, like banks, and universities. When people have difficult questions to answer, they go to the machines and they can solve even the most difficult problem in less than a second. There are lots of different types of computers, but they are always fast, and cost a lot of money.

' "But must computers be so large? Lots of other machines started off by being big, and have got smaller. This is true of things like radios and television sets, so why not computers? One day a computer might be small enough to carry about, so that everyone could have one, like they have a watch or a pen today.

' "Computers cannot reason like the human brain does. This means they can only answer with a yes or a no. But in the future, perhaps the computer could be joined on to the human brain, so that the two work together. I think in A.D. 2500 people might wear computers on their heads, so that they can think like they do now, but have the advantage of a computer's speed and memory to give them the best of both worlds.

' "My teacher has told me that different parts of the brain do different things. One part is for seeing, one part for the emotions, and so on. Nobody is quite sure about it yet, but in 500 years from now, they will have mapped out every bit of the brain, so each part could have its own computer. If that happened, the way men think might change. Not just get better and faster, but actually change into something different from the way our minds work today.

' "It might be possible to develop different parts of the brain, so that men can do things they cannot do now— such as telepathy.

' "If we saw someone with computers on his head, we would probably think it very strange and ugly. But to people in the future, it would seem as natural as wearing glasses".'

He looked up. 'That's the end.'

Grandfather took the magazine, put on his glasses, and read the whole thing for himself.

'Well, look at that. Your name at the top and everything.'

Tim felt a little bit embarrassed. 'The only thing is, I feel a bit of a cheat. I mean, everybody thinks I made it all up, but really it was just telling about Percy.'

'Never mind about that. It's your essay, not Percy's. It's not cheating to use what you know to your own advantage.'

'Don't you think so?' Tim was reassured.

'I think it's a very fine bit of writing.'

'It isn't really. I just wrote it down, didn't correct it or anything.'

'Well, you take it home and show your father. He's not seen it yet, I suppose?'

'No, he was away when it arrived. Mum said to take home your dirty washing.'

'That's good of her. Don't forget your pound.'

'You bet I won't. I'm going to have a look at cameras on Saturday.'

'It's a good thing to have.'

'And the first picture I take will be of—guess who?'

He laughed and went off home.

Mr Barnes stopped him after biology the next day.

'I've been meaning to ask you. How did you get the idea for your essay?'

'Oh, it sort of came to me one day when I was out for a walk,' he replied truthfully.

Before the competition, Tim had sometimes found it hard to make friends at school. The essay had changed all that. Everyone was friendly, and all the teachers knew him by name. After all, it had been worth going in for, just for the reputation it had given him. He found he was even enjoying his lessons more.

The weather was warm and sunny, not at all like November. Tim stayed out every evening, playing football or conkers with Victor and Ellen. Everything seemed to be back to normal; there were no more replies to their letters about Tribaxin. It seemed that the whole scientific world trusted Grand Universal Laboratories too much to take him seriously. Certainly the idea that a new plastic could turn into a deadly poison seemed to most of them the most ridiculous flight of fancy.

But sometimes Tim remembered. He felt again the pain and sadness of Percy. He tried to explain the feeling one day to Ellen. 'We were so *close*, El. It was like being inside his brain. But it was full of pain. It was like being in a room full of wailing.'

'You really did feel all of each other's emotions?'

'Just as if we were one person.'

She considered this, and then said slowly, 'I sometimes feel as if I know what other people are thinking. Just in flashes, you know. I can't prove it, but it's enough to make me see how you must feel.'

Their mother came into the room. 'Tim, you've got another letter from the magazine.'

'Fan mail,' Ellen grinned. 'Come on, open it.'

Tim opened the envelope.

'It isn't a fan letter. At least, I don't think so. They say a letter arrived for me, addressed to the magazine, and they've sent it to me.'

'Well what does it say?'

'Hang on, give me a chance! It says: "I have read your winning essay with a great deal of interest. It shows a knowledge and grasp of the research I am at present involved in, quite outside the normal grasp of a schoolboy. It raises doubts in my mind about the secrecy I had assumed surrounded my work, a project which you will understand is quite unique, and, to my knowledge, not being duplicated anywhere else in the scientific world."'

He stopped reading, and exchanged a surprised look with his mother.

'What does it mean?'

'It means this man, whoever he is, thinks you're pinching his secrets. Go on. There's more.'

' "I think it is imperative we meet, and would appreciate it if you would let me know when you are free to visit me at my laboratory in the near future." Signed Professor A. Hellebore.'

'Whatever will you do?' Ellen asked, aghast. 'He sounds ever so important. And ever so cross.'

'There's only one thing I can do—go and see him. And tell him it's just a coincidence.'

'Tim's right,' his mother said. 'He's got to be told face to face it's your own idea, and you haven't ever heard of him—otherwise he could get nasty.'

They looked at the address at the top of the page.

'Hellebore Laboratories, Ashdean, near Cambridge.'

'But, Tim, that's miles and miles from here. How ever will you get there?'

Tim didn't answer, but took the letter over to Grandfather's at the first moment he could.

'Well, you can't go on your own, that's for sure. You're daft enough to get lost between here and Shenton, let alone Cambridge. I'd better go along too.'

'Would you really? That would be great!'

'It's too far to get there and back in a day, anyway. We'd better ask the Professor to find us somewhere to stay the night.'

'When shall we go?'

'It will have to be a Saturday, because of your school. Anyway, where is it? Is it on the railway?'

'Let's go and ask at the station,' Ellen suggested

practically. She had come along too.

They were told by the local station-master that Ashdean was on a branch line from Cambridge. They were lucky; it was still open but due to be closed at the end of the year. They would have to go to London Bridge, across the City to Liverpool Street Station, and then catch another train to Cambridge. It would cost a lot of money, and when he said how much, Tim whistled.

'There goes my camera. It will cost even more if we have to stay in a boarding house overnight.'

Ellen was very angry for his sake. 'I think that Professor is mean to ask you to go so far. He knew you were only a schoolboy.'

'But he didn't know where I live,' Tim answered, reasonably. 'He wrote to the magazine, remember.'

'That makes it worse. You might have lived in the Outer Hebrides for all he cared. Anyway, I've got about four pounds in the post office you can have.'

'No. I won't take your money.'

'What about asking dad?'

Tim shook his head. 'It wouldn't seem right when I've got that five pounds already.'

His mother was cross about it, too. 'All that fuss and expense! Why couldn't he have offered to come here?'

'Never mind. I'll write off and tell him to expect me and Grandad next Saturday.'

'If Grandfather hadn't said he would go too, I'd not let you go after all.'

Tim listened to her grumbling for a few more minutes.

'Anyway, you'll have to have a new pair of trousers. Where's the money for those to come from, I'd like to know.'

'What do I need new trousers for? I've got trousers.'

'You can't wear those—they need turning down. You've grown so tall these last few weeks.'

Ellen cut in quickly. 'I'll turn them down, Mum, don't worry.'

Mrs Dunwoodie refused, but seemed more mollified. She had the last word, however. 'I don't know what your father will say when he comes home.'

'Hellebore?' Mr Dunwoodie said, very impressed when he read the letter. 'He's one of the most famous scientists we've got. A biochemist, I think he is.'

'All the more reason for Tim to look decent,' his wife said, taking down the sewing basket and moving to the window. 'Now, where are those grey trousers?'

'I'll write the letter, if you like,' Mr Dunwoodie said. 'What time did you say the train was?'

The Professor replied by return of post.

'Saturday would suit me very well,' he wrote. 'Any time of day will do, and you and your grandfather will be very welcome to stay overnight with me.'

That was one problem solved. And the Professor had solved another: inside his letter was a five pound note 'to help towards the fares' so Tim would not have to go without his camera, after all.

'He sounds quite a nice man,' he ventured to say to Ellen.

But privately he wondered about it. He had the sick feeling in his stomach all over again, like the day he had gone to Grand Universal. Still, he thought, he couldn't be much worse than Sir Arthur Bernard MacLeish.

13

Professor Hellebore

The hot journey to Ashdean Station finally ended at about half past three. It had taken a good part of the day to get there, because the trains ran to Ashdean only at three-hourly intervals, and they had a long wait at Cambridge for the branch line train. Tim was carrying a duffle bag with his pyjamas, toothbrush, and a clean shirt inside. He felt terribly hungry and thirsty, most of all thirsty. They had stopped at the station buffet for some ham rolls and tea, but that was all he had had since an early breakfast.

Grandfather wiped his forehead. He looked very cross. 'I hope this Professor of yours has got some tea on the go. Where's his letter?'

He took the paper out of his pocket and showed the address to the ticket collector.

'How far is it?' he asked, and the man pointed up the hill outside the station.

'Can't miss it, Guv'nor. Up on the right, a few huts set back from the road. The name's on the gate.'

It was good to stretch their legs and breath the cold air after the long stuffy train journey. They found the gate, just as the ticket collector had said, with its hand-painted notice: 'HELLEBORE LABORATORIES. PRIVATE.'

Tim looked at the three, shabby huts. What kind of a man could Professor Hellebore be? His father had said he was a famous man, but this did not look like a famous scientist's laboratory. It looked like an old army camp.

Grandfather knocked on the peeling door and gave Tim a wink of encouragement. Inside, they could hear a radio playing pop music, and somehow this made everything seem more normal. Then the door opened.

The Professor held out his hand, first to Grandfather and then to Tim. 'So you've arrived. I'm so glad.'

He was a very short, very wide man. At first, Tim took him to be fat, but later he realized it was a muscular body with no fat on it at all. He was wearing a dirty white coat, and looked about as shabby as his laboratories.

'I expect you're ready for tea. I've got the kettle on.'

Grandfather looked relieved and flopped on to a high stool.

'I don't often have visitors here. I only come here for my private work. Most people come to see me at the University.'

He chatted while he put out some doughnuts and buns on a plate and made the tea. 'If there were no buns, it would be necessary to invent them,' he said, and Tim wondered why Grandfather laughed—he did not see why it was funny.

He looked about him. Grand Universal had given him a glimpse of what a laboratory looked like, but it had been nothing like this. Everything was in an indescribable jumble; apart from everything being dusty, there were wires trailing everywhere, and he had to duck under some to find a seat. There were saucers full of screws and nails, and pots of glue and paint, and piles of magazines on the floor, and lots of strange-looking machinery that was not quite like radio and not quite like television. On one wall, a blackboard used for chemical symbols had scrawled in the corner: 'Remember the Dunwoodies'.

'What a super place,' Tim thought, and, forgetting to

be polite, helped himself to another bun and wandered about, poking into all the mysterious jumble.

The Professor and Grandfather seemed to be getting on together very well, and ignored Tim. He listened to the Professor answering a question about his work.

'This is my private work. Nothing to do with the University—I work here on my own. Some of the problems I'm tackling are very sticky . . .' He licked some sugar crumbs off his fingers as if to prove the point.

'When I read Tim's article, I really had quite a jolt. I had to see him to find out how he had hit on the same idea as myself—it seemed too incredible that he hadn't heard it from somebody, and if he had, I wanted to know. A security leak at this stage might mean months of work for nothing, do you see?'

His eyes were very keen as he looked at Tim. 'No one else in the world, as far as I know, is doing the same sort of work. So how you knew about it is a mystery.'

'Go on, Tim. You'd better tell the Professor about how it happened.'

'I didn't make it up, but you might think so when I tell what happened.'

So once again Tim launched on the story of Percy, and the strange computers he wore on his head. When he started to tell how they worked, the Professor stopped him.

'Tell me, what did they look like exactly? What colour were they?'

By his tone, Tim could see this was a crucial question. He thought very hard, and in his mind's eye he could see how Percy had looked, his bald head shining in the afternoon sun, and the headpieces wired into his head.

'They were sort of bluish, I think. Sort of like blue

glass. I could see through them and sometimes they seemed to light up.'

The Professor looked at the blackboard. 'Can you draw them for me?'

'I'll try.'

He took some chalk and drew a semicircle, with one side flat and the other slightly jagged. Then he added a line, and said, 'The wire sort of disappeared into his head. They looked like that.'

The Professor stared as if at some masterpiece.

'So that's how it is. Of course, they would be . . .' His voice trailed off, as lost in thought, he contemplated the chalked drawing. Then he clapped Tim fondly on the shoulder. 'Young man, I think you've saved me about six month's work. Like glass you say? Hmmm.'

He began walking round the laboratory in an excited fashion, and seemed quite to forget Tim and his grandfather. He lit a bunsen burner, which seemed to be the only form of heating in the place. Then he took up some wires and bits of metal. 'To work, then,' he said softly.

'But I haven't finished telling you the story yet,' Tim cut in hurriedly. 'The bit in the story that worries us so.'

All the time Tim was telling him the story of the poisoned sea, the Professor kept busy with the wires. He seemed to be only half listening.

'So, after seeing the Managing Director, and writing all the letters, we didn't know what else to do,' Tim finished.

There was quite a long silence, and he glanced at Grandfather for support. The old man was just finishing his fourth cup of tea, and slowly filled his pipe.

'What do you think, then, Professor?' he asked.

'Think? I think it is entirely likely that this Tribaxin

is the cause. Who can tell about these things? It might just as well be that as anything else.'

'I didn't mean that. I mean, what should we do now?'

'Nothing more you can do, I should think. Just hope they manage to sort it out for themselves in the future.'

There was another silence. Tim felt himself grow red with disappointment. He was not sure what he had expected; in fact, he did not know he had expected anything from the Professor until he saw how uninterested he seemed by the story. Then he realized he must have had an idea at the back of his mind that such an important man would somehow, miraculously, offer them the solution.

Grandfather got up and quietly stood by the Professor, as he still worked at the bench. He looked a little bit pink, too.

'It seems to me, Professor, that this is your fight now, as well as ours.'

He seemed surprised. 'How do you mean?'

'You seem to be very excited over what Tim has told you. Having Percy appear like that, and having him wearing these things on his head and all, has showed you aren't barking up the wrong tree. You said yourself, knowing what they look like might save you months of work.'

'That's true.'

'Well, my point is, you owe him, this Percy, something in return.'

Hellebore put down the wires, and thought about what Grandfather had said. He sighed regretfully, but nodded in agreement. 'First things first, eh?'

'There'll be plenty of time for your computers,' Grandfather said equably. 'But just now, it would be very nice to have your help on the poisoning.'

'But I know nothing about plastics. Or the sea, for that matter.'

'Someone you know, perhaps?'

He thought for a while. Then he said, 'Pandie would be a good man, but he's in America. Cudlipp—no, he died last week. Bremlin and Todd are up the Amazon. Can't think of anybody else.'

He fixed his eyes again on the workbench. 'I suppose a name will spring to mind.'

Tim could not stop himself. Suddenly he burst out, 'We don't know anything about plastics, either! But we're trying to do something to help Percy and the dolphins and everybody! You *must* know someone.'

The Professor looked at Tim with a new respect. The boy's concern had touched him at last.

'Perhaps the Minister can suggest someone—I'm dining with him this evening, in fact.'

'The Minister?' Grandfather asked breathlessly. 'What Minister?'

'The Minister of Science and Technology.' The Professor suddenly chuckled. 'Every now and then I go to see him, and he promises me another three bob's worth of wire. We both get rude—but we're old friends, really.'

Tim could hardly stand the coolness of the man.

'But don't you see? He's the very man to help!'

'Do you think so? Perhaps you're right. A man with power might be more help than a man with knowledge at this juncture. And if you want power, don't come to me, or any other scientist, or the University for that matter. It's the Government that cracks the whip.'

'Hear hear,' said Grandfather, as if he were at a political meeting. Tim had not followed this little speech very well, but he saw the Professor was now willing to do something to help, and that was enough. He was flooded with a new hope.

'Perhaps we'd better go now. The traffic can be very bad at this time of the evening.'

It took Tim a moment to realize he meant that they were to go with him, to the Minister's house.

'Won't he mind?' he asked.

'He might.' The Professor's face lit up with amusement. He looked a nicer, warmer man all of a sudden. 'But it would do him good to meet someone like you for a change—someone with spunk.'

'Come on, then,' Grandfather cut in. 'Don't forget your duffle bag.' And he added under his breath, 'Mind your manners when we get there, for goodness sake!'

A little bewildered, the two of them followed Professor Hellebore out of the hut, and wondered where they were to go: they had no idea where the Minister lived.

'I hope we don't have to go on another train. I've had quite enough for one day,' Grandfather whispered.

The Professor, however, led them to one of the other rusty huts, which turned out to be his garage. After the splendid cars Tim had seen outside Grand Universal, he felt a certain excitement. Professor Hellebore would have a very special car, he was sure—perhaps even a Rolls Royce.

From inside the garage came a great bang and mechanical cough, and then the Professor slowly drove his car out for them to see. Grandfather put on his glasses to have a better look. He sighed nostalgically.

'What a beauty! 1931 Bullnose, isn't it?'

'Had it practically all my life,' the Professor agreed, as they climbed in. 'Still got the original brasswork.'

'Had one myself, when I was younger,' Grandfather said proudly. Then they were off, and Tim listened to their talk about carburettors, petrol consumption, transmission and hub caps for what seemed like miles and miles.

Half an hour later, although it seemed like more, he wondered if they would ever get to wherever they were going. The old car was croaking its way up every little hill, as if on its last gasp. It was very bumpy in the back seat, and he felt slightly sick. He bent forward to exchange a word with Grandfather, but found he had his eyes shut and looked a little bit green, so perhaps he was feeling sick too. Tim leaned back in the shuddering, bumpy old car and tried to think hard about anything but being sick. And at last the Professor signalled with his arm to turn left and slowed down.

'We're there,' he said.

14

At the Minister's

They drove into the drive of a beautiful house.

Thankfully, Grandfather heaved himself out of the car. 'That will teach me to feel nostalgic,' he said to Tim.

'At least we arrived. I began to think we wouldn't.'

It was full night-time now. A small moon appeared and disappeared as clouds chased across the sky. An owl hooted away to their left in some trees, and there was a hint of frost in the air. From the house, bright warm light streamed from nearly all the windows, and it looked cosy and welcoming.

The front door was at the top of a small flight of steps, and it was opened almost at once by a butler—the first one Tim had ever seen outside films.

If he felt any surprise at the sight of Professor Hellebore's companions, he managed not to show it. He bade them good evening and ushered the trio into the Minister's study. He told the cook a little later that there were two more scruffy-looking scientists for dinner.

'He's expecting you, Professor,' he said, allowing himself very slightly to emphasize the 'you'. The Professor had already flung open the door, however, and announced his own arrival. 'Here I am, George,' he called pleasantly, 'come to cadge a few more bits of wire.'

It did not occur to Tim at the time that this was a long-standing joke between them; he felt himself blushing at what he thought was the Professor's rudeness.

But the Minister laughed. All he said was, 'We'll see about that, Alfred.'

The Minister of Science and Technology was a tall, distinguished looking man in early middle age. Tim knew his face, he realized, from television interviews and photographs in the newspapers. In real life he looked thinner and more kind.

'Here are two new friends of mine,' said the Professor. 'Hope you don't mind me bringing them along. Mr and Master Dunwoodie.'

'Delighted to have you come,' the Minister answered. He rang a small bell on his desk, and the butler appeared silently at the door.

'Tell cook there will be two more to dinner,' was all he said, and then turned graciously back to his guests.

Tim felt grubby and untidy. He had never been in such a grand house. The furniture was beautiful, and the gleaming silver and gilded picture frames gleamed in the light of a large, log fire. The Professor did not look exactly smart, either. He had taken off his dirty laboratory coat, but underneath he was only wearing a roll necked pullover and a pair of old, tweed trousers. It would have been nice, too, if Grandfather had worn a tie with no egg stains on it.

It was a great relief when the Minister said, 'I'm sure you all feel a bit dusty after your journey,' and showed them to a cloakroom, where they got busy with large, expensive bars of soap, clean towels and clothes brushes. Tim brushed his hair for the first time that day, and it was an altogether neater looking trio that emerged. The

97

Minister poured drinks for them all while he talked.

'What can I give you, Master Dunwoodie? Orange juice with soda is rather nice. And for you, Mr Dunwoodie? Ale? Certainly, unless you'd rather have some sherry. No?'

The Professor had some sherry, and the Minister took a small glass of madeira.

'Cheerio,' said Grandfather, and drank his ale down with a sigh of content. There was a small silence.

The Professor turned to the Minister. 'What did the Committee have to say?'

'I don't think you have to worry. They seem to think the work worth a grant. One or two doubted if you would get results very soon.'

'They'll get results all right—perhaps sooner than they think,' he said, and smiled secretly at Tim.

The Minister saw the smile, but said nothing. There came the sound of a gong, which meant dinner was served, so they all got up and went into the dining room.

The table was lit with two silver candelabra, and the knives and forks were heavy silver too. Grandfather winked at Tim, as if to say, 'Look at this, isn't it posh?'

The meal was just as grand as they had been led to expect. There were bowls of creamy soup, then trout, then venison steaks. Tim had never eaten venison before and thought it was quite delicious. He was given two glasses of wine with a little water added. The Minister looked at him and Grandfather a little curiously at times, but talked to the Professor about scientific friends, new discoveries in biochemistry, the disastrous cricket season. Obviously, if the Professor did not want to explain why he had brought the two along, the Minister was much too polite to ask.

After two helpings of strawberry trifle, Tim went with the three men back to the study for coffee.

Grandfather sat down in the corner. He could not keep his eyes open any longer. Tired from all the travelling and excitement of the day, unaccustomed to wine and large meals at such a late hour, the old man slumped further and further down in his chair, until a faint snore betrayed he had fallen asleep.

'He doesn't often have such a hard day,' Tim said to the Minister, defensively. 'We've been travelling since seven o'clock this morning.'

The Minister smiled sympathetically and looked at

Grandfather. His hand caressed the head of an old Labrador, stretched out at his feet, also asleep.

'You've come a long way, then?'

The question was put in such a way that either a straightforward denial or agreement could be given, or a fuller explanation. Tim looked at his grandfather, then at the Professor, who simply gave a brief nod. One thing Tim was learning about Professor Hellebore—he always expected people to stand on their own feet, and he treated Tim, not as a young boy in need of help and protection, but just as he would treat another adult.

Tim did not feel at all like an adult just then. The large meal, the long day, the wine, all helped to make everything seem unreal. He could not concentrate on what he had to say. Yet he knew this was the chance he had been waiting for, his great opportunity to help Percy and Beppo. He searched in his mind for words that might sway the Minister into helping him, words that would make him see what a terrible burden Tim had had to carry.

'Percy!' he thought despairingly. 'If only you were here. You would know what to say!' But Percy was not there. He had to do what he could, on his own.

'Yes, we have come a long way,' he finally answered. 'The Professor wrote to me and asked me to come and see him, because he thought I knew too much about his work. But that isn't why we came here, it's just part of it. You see, I've got to stop us from poisoning the sea.'

He stopped. The Minister, head on one side in polite encouragement, looked completely baffled.

Almost shaking with effort, Tim plunged on. 'About a month ago, I saw a boy. He said he was from the future. He *was* from the future, and he wore things on his head like the Professor is trying to make.'

'More or less the same,' was all the Professor said.

'Go on,' prompted the Minister.

'He told me the sea was poisoned and his dolphin was going to die.'

'His dolphin?'

'The whole question of ecology is most neglected, don't you think?' the Professor said to no one in particular.

Tim did not know what ecology was, or whether it would help Beppo if he did. 'This boy told me, later on, that they thought the thing poisoning the sea was something called Tribaxin. And then I found out Tribaxin was a new plastic. And a boat sank in the Atlantic with Tribaxin inside. So now I'm sure that's what done it.'

He blushed. The Minister would think him an ignorant little boy now, who could not even speak English properly. 'Did it, I mean.'

The Minister was still showing the same polite attention, whatever his thoughts might have been.

'Tribaxin? Yes, I've heard of it. Surely the makers have tested it? It's being made by a very reputable firm. Have you—have your family—contacted them?'

'I have. They said it couldn't possibly be Tribaxin. They said it is tested for everything.'

'What an extraordinary story.' The Minister spoke very kindly, but there was a note of finality in his voice as if to hint that he was a busy man and must not waste time on fairy stories. 'If the manufacturers are sure it isn't Tribaxin, then the poison the boy told you about must come from something else.'

Tim felt tears of exhaustion and self pity pricking his eyes, but he was determined not to cry. He realized he had had the most marvellous chance, and he had failed.

There was nothing more he could do. Grandfather slept on; the Professor said nothing.

'Why doesn't he say something?' Tim thought bitterly. 'He might at least try to help convince the Minister.'

But the Professor did not intervene. He did not seem to think the battle an uneven one—he expected a little boy to convince a powerful, busy Minister of Science on his story's merits.

Tim looked at their kind, distant faces, then at the fire. It blurred and jumped with the tears he held back, and waves of desolation prevented him from saying anything more at all.

15

The Return of Percy

Tim felt like a general who had just lost the war. The Minister sat beside him, totally unconvinced by the story he had heard. Tim could not blame him for that—he had not even told it well. After all, if an unknown, not very well-educated, boy suddenly appears at your house to dinner, claims to have seen into the future, and without any proof at all expects the Minister of *Science* to believe him, well, he is asking for trouble.

These were Tim's bitter thoughts as they sat on in the Minister's study. Each of them was sunk in his own thoughts. The dog whimpered and shivered in his sleep; Grandfather twitched uneasily; a log fell with a shower of sparks further into the fire.

'It seems very cold all of a sudden,' the Minister exclaimed, getting up to put more logs on the fire. As he reached towards the firetongs, a chilly wind seemed to touch them all, blowing from every direction and yet from nowhere. The corners of the room seemed to fade away, until the four of them and the dog were enclosed in a ball of light that throbbed and shimmered all around them. It was as if they were trapped in a huge pearl, and a sensation of cold and shimmering light seemed to pass through them all for a second, three seconds, perhaps an hour. They had lost all sense of time. Even the Professor, trained to observe facts scientifically, had to confess afterwards that the clock seemed to blur and fade before his eyes, and even his own heartbeats were still.

The frozen figures gaped at each other, not able to move or speak. Then, gradually, a warm, natural light returned. The slight noises of the room—the clock and the fire—could be heard again. It was no longer cold.

The Minister dropped the fire tongs he had been holding and everything seemed as natural as it had a few moments (hours?) before.

Except for one thing. Percy was sitting on the sofa.

He grinned, a conspiratorial and encouraging grin, at Tim. Then he stood up and bowed politely, first to the Minister and then to Professor Hellebore. His bald head and the headpieces flashed and gleamed in the firelight.

'Greetings. Please forgive me for intruding, but the Elders thought it might be necessary. They have sent me here to help my friend.' He glanced at Tim whose heart was leaping about in his chest with sheer joy.

'Oh, Percy, I'm so glad to see you!' he exclaimed.

The Minister closed his mouth, which had been gaping foolishly, and managed to stammer a welcome. The Professor took hardly any notice of anything that was said. Eyes popping, he stared at Percy's microcybs.

'When I last saw Tim,' Percy was saying, 'my arrival was purely accidental. A combination of faults in two of the microcybs projected me to your present and my past, and so we met.'

'So he has said,' stuttered the Minister.

'Of course, coming back again to the correct time was very difficult. What was once done by error had to be reprocessed deliberately.'

The Professor nodded vigorously. 'Scientific progress is often like that. A mistake, an accident, opens up a new field. Then you have to find out what you actually *did* to make the discovery.'

Percy laughed. He was standing now in front of the fire, graceful and at ease. There was nothing of the young, inadequate boy about *him*. He spoke to them all as equals.

'I want to tell you, Professor Hellebore, that your time is known to us as the Age of Amateurs. We know that many of the discoveries you made were random and unplanned, just as we know they led to many unplanned and evil side effects. They were mere stabs in the dark. We, in our time, are not used to dealing in—errors.'

The Professor looked furious, then sulky. He did not like to be called an amateur. After a moment's reflection, however, he saw that Percy had not meant to be rude. He had simply said the truth as he saw it.

'I won't quarrel with you, young man. But you must have repeated your error, all the same, otherwise you wouldn't have appeared just now.'

Percy shook his head. 'No. We found it impossible to transfer again.'

The others looked at him in surprise.

'How did you get here, then?' Tim asked. 'If you couldn't do it, how did you manage it?'

Percy grinned at him again. 'First of all, you must understand that I am not *here*. Not really. The real me is still in my own time. I am some sort of mirror image of myself, rather like a beam of light, or a thought, but I don't expect you to understand.'

'Telepathy is the nearest word we have,' the Minister said.

Percy nodded. 'That too. Let me explain how I came. I did not come by the power of my own brain—and certainly it was no error this time.'

He sat comfortably next to Tim, and began to tell them some of the difficult times he had had since his last meeting with Tim. In some ways it was a repetition of his friend's: he had found it difficult to convince people it had really happened, and that a contact with the past had been made. Of course, he found it was made easier for him by using his telecyb, and opening his mind up to those around him. Some of the experiences he had had with Tim could be 'read' telepathically. He had tried to convince his parents and his teachers how important it would be if he could only go back again to try and stop the manufacture of Tribaxin. His family had seen it as a waste of his brain's energies, just at the time he needed to concentrate most on his Big Examinations. And his teachers pointed out that, as the poisoning had already happened, and was in their seas, it was too late to do anything by going back again. The fish were dead, the dolphins dying. The poison existed. But Percy was obstinate. By huge efforts of will, entirely on his own, he had somehow contacted Tim with just those few words: 'Tribaxin, Tim, Tribaxin'. But he could not manage any more.

He went on, 'My own power was limited, but I could not believe there was nothing else I could do. You see, my pet dolphin, Beppo, was dying.'

They were all engulfed with the boy's tender love and grief for his dolphin. The Minister instinctively reached out and caressed the head of his dog, who thumped his tail twice, although he was still asleep.

Grandfather slept on as well. It was very strange, he

told Tim afterwards, but he remembered every second of the visit from Percy, just as if it had been a most vivid dream. Sleep, apparently, was no barrier to this particular form of telepathy.

'Whatever did you do?' the Professor asked, hoarsely. He was obviously moved by the strength of Percy's pain.

'I managed to gain an interview with one of the Elders. He listened to me most kindly. He also told me I could not alter the course of history. The poison, he said, existed. I could not make it cease to exist.'

Percy seemed to blur and waver before them, as if he was tiring. Then he became clear and distinct again.

He continued, 'I must not talk too much about the Elders. This will be understood by you when I explain how it is I am with you.

'The Elder I spoke to took me to four others. Between them they came to a decision which gave me a final chance. The Elders do not wear microcybs, but can do many things without them. They are different, and understand things more than we do. Together they are giving me the power to come back to you. In fact, the five Elders are standing round me now as I talk, and as you think I am with you. They say it could not be done without my own special strength. They say it has to be me that speaks to you, because of my attachment to Beppo. Do you see? I care so much about him, I'd do anything to save him.'

They did see. All of them knew the power of love.

'So the Elders don't want me to speak about them, for that would bring their thoughts into the room as well as my own. They say this could not help solve the problem. They are quite firm about it.' He spoke as if he were listening to another voice giving him directions.

'So you are here because of the Elders, and not because of the microcybs?'

'Precisely.'

'How did you find me?' Tim asked, puzzled. 'I'm nowhere near the Dell—even *I* don't know where I am, exactly.'

'Where you were did not matter, once your individual personality had been "read" by the Elders from my telepathic picture of you. Everyone is unique. That means there never has been, nor ever will be, anyone quite like you. They found you, because you are the only Tim Dunwoodie.'

Percy waited, as if he expected more questions. Indeed, all of them were dying to find out as much as possible before the inevitable time came for Percy to fade away. The Minister spoke next.

'Forgive me for asking a question which may offend the Elders. I think it may only bring them in indirectly. What I should like to know is, what kind of government do you have in your day? Are decisions and laws made by the Elders?'

Percy shook his head. 'Oh, no. The Elders are not representatives of anybody. They are just themselves. They serve just by thinking, and anyone can ask their advice. Our government is sort of like yours. But since the use of telepathy, the way we choose our representatives has had to change.'

'Why is that?'

'In your time, Minister, there were two main parties, and one made the laws while the others tried to stop them, or change them. Right?'

'That's right,' he agreed.

Percy looked as if he was enjoying himself. 'Often,

each representative made promises to get elected, and he said many fine things. In their hearts, they thought something quite different. Their words were sweet, their hearts cunning. To gain power, they were prepared to tell lies. Is this true?'

'Well . . .' The Minister did not know what to say.

Percy laughed. 'Oh, I know you don't lie, Minister. And I'm sure there are more honest men than dishonest ones, even in your Parliament.'

The Minister looked uneasy, just as the Professor had a little time earlier, when he had been called an amateur. But in the end, he too agreed that Percy was right.

'When telecybs were invented, do you see, men could not gain office by saying one thing and thinking another. This was true about the Government, and business men and just about everybody. They had to use new criteria for electing leaders or representatives. The things that matter now are things like wisdom, concern for others, honesty and intelligence. Speech-making no longer counts. So I think you can see,' Percy finished, a little slyly, 'our choices are a little different from yours.'

The Minister shook his head as if to clear it, and then joined in the laugh that the Professor had started.

'Absolutely fascinating! No more cunning old foxes in Parliament! What a prospect—but where do they all go?'

They all laughed again. 'There aren't so many of them now. If you can't lie to gain your own ends, then you soon learn to become honest.'

The Professor leaned forward to gain Percy's attention.

'Please, may I ask you a question? About the micro-cybs?'

'I think so.'

'Why do they glow and wink in that way?'

'It's the energy produced in the heliostites.'

'Heliostites?'

'Oh, of course, you haven't discovered them yet.'

He shook his head regretfully, and although the Professor pleaded with him to tell him how to make them, Percy stayed firm.

'I cannot say anything that is going to help you too much in the future. Surely you can see that that would be tampering with history. And I mustn't do that.'

'But you've been telling the Minister all about your Government.' The Professor almost wailed with disappointment.

'No, really, I haven't said anything that would change history. All I have said about telepathy would have occurred to all of you, given time and common sense. It would be quite different to reveal scientific formulae.'

And nothing the Professor said would make him budge an inch.

Tim now found a chance to put in his questions. He knew there were a million things he would wish he had asked when it was too late, but while they were together, all he really wanted to know about were things to do with Percy himself.

'How's Beppo? Is he all right?'

Percy was able to smile, although a little sadly, and answered that Beppo was only a little worse than he had been before.

'And, Percy, what do you want to be when you grow up?'

Percy's image blurred a little, but he answered clearly enough. 'I want to be an Elder. I know, of course, you can't *try* to be one. Either one's brain develops along certain lines or it doesn't. You can't make it happen.'

Percy thought a little more. 'When we met before, I told you how I feel about the sea and the dolphins. I just about remember what the sea used to be like, before the poison. It's only possible now in the Pacific and parts of the Indian Ocean to go on with scientific research, and seabed farming. Still, I would like one day to do something like that—be an oceanographer.'

They had all asked Percy questions. They sat in silence, remembering why they were all together. His talk of the sea had reminded them.

'So all the seas aren't poisoned yet?'

'Not yet. The Pacific is almost completely free of it, and only parts of the China Seas and Indian Ocean are affected. Which is just as well,' Percy added wryly, 'because most of the food eaten in Asia comes from the sea. When—if—the poison reaches that far, millions of people may starve.'

The Minister spoke quietly. 'You are sure it is this Tribaxin?'

'We are. It is filtering out from somewhere in the Atlantic, following the currents.'

'But it has been tested.' The Professor's protest sounded feeble, even to his own ears.

'I wish that were true,' Percy burst out passionately. 'Has it been tested to see what happens when it is left in the sea for five hundred years? Has it? That's what we mean by things being only half done, half guessed at, in your time. I wish I had time to tell you about all the other of your inventions and actions that have caused trouble in the time between you and me.'

'The Age of Amateurs,' the Professor said grimly.

'Yes. And who knows how much pain and suffering you have inflicted because you are just that.'

'Percy,' the Minister said. 'That isn't quite fair. It's always easy after the event to see who was the culprit. We do our best, and we make mistakes. We shall make less mistakes, I hope, as time goes on, because there will always be people who care about the world, and who will be concerned about putting things right. You talk as if everyone in the past were careless or stupid or downright bad. But we aren't. If we were, where would the foundation stones for a better future come from? Who would make the jump from bad to good in one leap? No one! You know that as well as I do. That isn't the way men work—every act leads to the next act, and we are all part of a chain from the past to the future. We make mistakes. We try to put them right. That's what being a human being is all about, at least it seems so to me.'

If it were possible for a telepathic projection to blush, Percy was blushing now.

'Do forgive me,' he said humbly. 'You are right. Mistakes are always possible. Otherwise we should not be men but—something else.'

Tim wondered if he was going to say, 'Machines' or perhaps 'Gods'. It would have been interesting to know. Percy did not give him the chance to ask, however, as he went on speaking intensely to the Minister.

'When I attacked you in that rude way, it was because of the pain I feel about the poisoned sea. You have not seen it, I have. Every day the beaches are black and stinking from the dead things. The dolphins,' Percy swallowed, 'lie bloated and suffering, along with other fish, waiting for their time to die.'

'I didn't tell the Minister about the dolphins,' Tim said quickly. 'He doesn't really know how important they are to you.'

'I'll tell him, then. The story starts about four hundred years ago, when men started using dolphins as sea carriers and messengers, because they could be trained to find "home", like carrier pigeons do in your time. The bonds between the dolphin and men became very strong. They were loving and intelligent, and learned quickly. Their thinking capacity grew remarkably as new demands were made of them, and only the barrier of language kept the dolphins from being true friends and equals.

'Then, fifty or so years ago, a telepathic microcyb was devised, which made "speech" between man and dolphin possible. Because the dolphins were wise about the sea, they helped men to find new places to grow food, and this teamwork grew until the poison started, about five years ago. Everyone who lives near the sea, as I do, has a pet dolphin. They teach us to swim and tell us stories about the sea. They love telling stories. My own pet, Beppo, is living in a tank now, in my garden. It's only now that we realize how important it is for the dolphins to be part of their own communities, telling each other stories and living together. He needs the sea and he needs other dolphins. Without them he is going to die.'

The Professor got up suddenly. He looked very angry. The story seemed to have affected him deeply.

'Come on, George. Get off your backside and do something!'

The Minister nodded. But he still wanted to ask Percy something else. 'The Tribaxin, Percy, do you think your own scientists will find a way to stop it spreading?'

'They don't know. They think it may die out of its own accord, if there isn't too much of it.'

'I promise you, and your Elders, that I will do all I can,

all I can,' he repeated, 'to stop any more of the Tribaxin being made. Some of it may get thrown in the sea, some of it has already been sent abroad. But I will see no more is made, and all the stocks in this country will be destroyed.'

He got up from his chair and walked over to a table where the telephone stood.

'Can you stay with us a little while longer?' he asked, as casually as if he were the boy living next door, but his meaning was clear. How long could the Elders use their strength to project Percy back in time?

'I can stay a little while longer. Everything is all right here. Your words have given the Elders new heart. Also,' he added charmingly, 'they say there is no barrier here to fight against, which would exhaust them. You are all receptive and kind.'

'Thank you,' the Minister said, pleased. 'Now, I won't be a moment.'

He dialled a number and spoke softly for a few minutes. The voice at the other end (was it the Prime Minister?) gave him the necessary permission. He then dialled another number, and spoke in sharper tones to somebody else.

Then he turned to Percy and smiled. 'There, that's settled. I'll make sure about the stocks being destroyed tomorrow. And we shall get international agreement about any dumping in the sea.'

So, with two phone calls, the Minister set in motion the events which he later referred to as 'tying up the loose end', and which Tim described to Ellen as 'The Two Telephone Calls that Changed the Course of History'.

16
The Dolphins

'There,' the Minister said kindly to Percy, 'your dolphin should be safe now. If only your scientists can contain this phase of the poisoning, there won't be any more.'

A beam of happiness seem to emanate from Percy. He could not speak, but, of course, they could all feel his relief and hope.

'I'm interested in this use of dolphins,' the Professor mused.

'First time you've shown any,' Tim thought.

'What a difference these telecybs must make to their brains. How much do you communicate?'

'I know Beppo so well, I already had a good idea what he was feeling, even before he started to wear telecybs. Now, of course, it's practically like speaking. Before he got ill, he could always sense my mood, and when I was miserable, he used to clown about and squeak, and look so funny I just had to laugh.'

'Wonderful, wonderful. And you say they need the company of other dolphins? To stay happy?'

'Yes. We found they had quite a complicated society amongst themselves, and without some contact with it, they got restless and depressed easily.'

'Something to do with the dancing?' Tim put in.

'What dancing?' asked the Professor.

Percy tried to explain. 'You have ballet, don't you? There aren't any words, but as long as the dancers are good, you can understand just what the ballet is about. Well, the dolphins *dance* their society. Perhaps the right way of putting it is to say they dance their myths. We think it's been going on since—since dolphins began to live in schools. It was discovered by a man—oh, I forgot, I mustn't give you his name. He spent nearly all his life, just watching the dolphins. He learned what their movements meant.'

'Percy,' Tim begged. 'Tell us a dolphin story. Then we'll understand them so much better. You can do that— I mean, are you allowed to tell us that?'

'I should love to! But first of all, I shall have to explain a bit about their background.'

Just then, Grandfather woke up with a start. They waited to see how he would react to Percy, in case it gave him a shock. But he smiled and nodded and told them he had heard every word that Percy had said, 'and I'm damn pleased to see it wasn't a dream. That means you've really done something about the Tribaxin?' he asked the Minister.

'Yes, it's all fixed. And now, Percy here is going to tell us a story about the dolphins. Before he starts, let me just ring for—' the Minister stopped himself and shrugged his shoulders with a small laugh. 'I was going to say, let me get us all a drink or a cup of tea, but I suppose under the circumstances I'd better not ask my butler in.'

So they settled down to hear the story.

'You may know,' Percy began, 'that the whales and the dolphins are thought to have come from the land some time millions and millions of years ago. They were probably a kind of grass-eating animal.'

'Like cows?' Tim asked with disbelief.

'That's right. As much like cows as anything. But we can't know for sure. The dolphins seem to have an idea they came from the land, and this story is about how it happened.

'This man I was telling you about, who studied the dolphins, watched them do the same dance, over and over again. It seemed to be quite an important one, because there were always crowds of them there to watch, and it was danced by the biggest and most important members of the school. Well, what he saw was this. The biggest male and his mate would dance in a circle, followed by the strongest young male dolphin. Another dolphin joined them, a big female, and she seemed to try and take the young male away. Then the two big leaders would stand on their tails (have you seen them do that?) and make squeaking noises—rather anxious noises. The male, the young one, went off a little way with the other female one, and whenever he tried to get back to the two standing dolphins, she would prevent him. He tried to get back three times. The standing dolphins were joined by all the others in a circle, and they all stood up and squeaked at him. But the other female would never let him get to them. Then he did manage to get back to the others. They all stayed together and slowly circled round and round. Then their dance got faster and faster, until the water foamed and swirled with their beating tails. They kept this up until the sea was a mass of white, then they all got back into the standing position and slowly disappeared under the waves.

'That wasn't the end. The young dolphin then did a frantic dance round the older female who had taken him away in the first place. Then all the other dolphins joined them, and swam about looking joyful. But the two older ones, the leaders who had stood up at the beginning, swam off a little way on their own, and kept leaping and leaping in the air, until they finally seemed so exhausted that three or four of the others went over to hold them up on their backs, just as if they had died. Then that was the end.'

Tim was terribly disappointed.

'That's not much of a story,' he could not help saying.

Percy smiled at him. 'Don't be silly. That's not the *story*. That's just the movements, the patterns that told the story to the man.'

'Do you see, Tim,' the Professor said, 'it's like trying to understand a ballet if you are just told what the steps are. The dancer may be said to do a leap in the air, and then an *entrechat*, but what you understand at the end of the dance is far more than that.'

'Exactly,' Percy agreed. 'I've told you the pattern. Now we put on the drama, the myth.'

'But how do you know you're right?' Tim pursued. 'What the man says it meant and what the dolphins might think it meant are two different things.'

Percy looked irritated. 'Do you like music? Do you ever listen to music?'

'Yes.' Tim nodded hesitatingly. 'Not much, but sometimes I like to.'

'How do you know that what you understand from the music is exactly what the composer meant?'

Tim felt stupid. 'Well, I don't know. I just get what I can out of it.'

'And does it really matter if what you get out of it and what the composer meant are exactly the same?'

'Well, no, I suppose it doesn't.'

'Then try and understand that what sense we make of the dolphin's dance may be different from what they meant, but it doesn't matter. It is enough that we can see it has *some* meaning in their lives.'

'Sorry,' Tim said humbly. Really, Percy did make him feel foolish at times. He tried not to catch anybody's eye.

Surprisingly, the Professor spoke up in his favour.

'I was just going to ask the same question myself, I must admit. So what we are going to hear is not a dolphin story, but a human story. That's not the same thing at all.'

'Until we can find a dolphin that speaks English or Dutch or Portugese, then it's got to be a human story, I can't dance it for you, or squeak like a dolphin,' Percy retorted.

'Do go on,' the Minister begged, trying to unruffle everybody's feelings. 'Of course we have to interpret the story in human terms. After all, the dolphin's world is totally different from our own. And without the use of words, the story must mean something quite different to them. But we understand that, don't we?'

They nodded or grunted in agreement, so Percy continued with the story.

'I said this dance was supposed to be about the origins of the dolphins. They do this dance all over the world, each school dances it at least twice a year. Sometimes the leaders, the two who get so exhausted at the end, are so carried away by what they are doing, that they have been known to kill themselves by throwing themselves up on a beach, too high for the others to rescue them.'

Tim felt a thrill of excitement, for he had heard of

dolphins doing this before. 'I've heard of whales doing that, too,' he said eagerly.

'Yes. The same dance is done by the whales, only they only do it in threes and fours.'

'Let him get on with the story,' Grandfather cut in.

'Well, here it is. A long, long time ago, between big lands, there was a country inhabited by the dolphins. They were gentle and intelligent, and walked on their hind legs. They cared for their young until they were old enough to get married themselves, and they lived together in peace.

'They had a king and a queen. Their son was a fine, strong prince, the joy of his mother and father, and of all the other dolphins, because he was fair and graceful and wise, just as his parents were. When they met together, the prince would lead the dance, and he would lead their young along the sea shore, because they all loved the sea.

'One day, the wicked queen of the sea saw him, when she was swimming near the dolphin's shores. The sound of his sweet singing drew her near, and when she saw him, she was filled with longing. Nothing would please her except to take him away with her to the bottom of the sea, where she would make him her husband. So, one day when the prince was swimming in the sea, and his parents were watching him from the beach, the wicked queen caused a strong wave to wash over him and bear him down to her palace at the bottom of the sea. She put on the disguise of a beautiful girl dolphin, and watched him with hungry, green eyes. The prince fell in love with her false image, and stayed, quite forgetting about his father and mother and the dolphin kingdom up above. She showed him her treasures of jewels and pearls, and he danced and sang to her for many a long day.

'But soon his need for the other dolphins made him long to return. He began to fret and pine. "You must stay with me!" she cried in a rage. "I'll not let you go."

'But the Prince escaped from her in the dark of night, and tried to get back to his home. But just before he reached the shore, the wicked queen of the sea awoke, and realized what had happened. She caused a magic net to be stretched all around him, and he was caught. He called and called for help from his mother and father, but nobody heard him, and he was dragged back to the palace under the sea.

'The next night, again he tried to escape. But again the sea queen woke up, and this time sent a great tidal wave to sweep him back to her palace. On the third night the prince was stopped by a mighty whirlpool, when he was only fifty feet away from the shore. But his mother had heard his cries. She was sure it was her son, and so she went to the beach every night to see if he would return.

'On the fourth night, she saw him coming through the waves, and she saw a silver net stretching all around him. She called to him and threw him the knife that she wore at her belt. He managed to cut a hole large enough to get through, and so he was able to swim safely to the shore.

'The dolphins had given him up for lost, and when they heard that their prince had returned, there was great rejoicing and feasting.

' "We will not allow him anywhere near the sea," the king said. "We will never allow him out of our sight, and the queen of the sea will not be able to catch him again."

'She, of course, was furious. She lashed the shores with

fierce waves and storms, so that the island was constantly covered with storms and hurricanes. It rained for a whole year, but the dolphins kept the young prince safe. They grew hungrier and hungrier, because the land was flooded and they could not find any grass to eat. And it continued to rain.

' "Let me go back," the prince pleaded. "I don't want you all to die of hunger for my sake."

'But they would not let him go. The queen of the sea grew angrier and angrier, and sent a huge wave, as high as the highest mountain, to wash all the dolphins into the sea, so she could get her prince back. When the waters closed over the dolphins, it swamped their land as well, and they, and their country, disappeared under the ocean.

'So the queen of the sea had her way. She took the prince down to her kingdom, and he said he would stay with here there for ever, if she would make one promise. She agreed. He said she must change all the dolphins into fish, so they would not die, and she must let him spend half his time with them, otherwise he would die himself from unhappiness. So she turned the dolphins into a kind of fish, all except the king and the queen, whom she did not trust to leave her and the prince alone. They struggled to save themselves by swimming to another country, but in the end, tired and half drowned, they succumbed to the waves.

'The dolphins found their bodies, and sadly carried them back to the prince. He wept for his mother and father. "Take their bodies to a dry land," he said. So they sadly took their old queen and king to a rocky shore and left them in the sun and the air.

'Perhaps the prince died of a broken heart, when he

found how the queen of the sea had broken her promise. Or perhaps he is living in her kingdom still, and one day will find the dolphins a new land, and release them from their fishy form.

'And that is the end of the story,' said Percy.

Tim felt exhilarated and at the same time a little sad. 'It's a lovely story. Do you know any more?'

'Lots,' Percy laughed. 'All about humans, and monsters of the deep, and giant squids. But I can't tell you any more.'

And then Tim noticed that Percy was beginning to fade.

'Oh, no,' he pleaded, close to tears. 'Please don't go yet. Please stay a little bit longer.'

'I have to go, friend,' Percy said faintly, regretfully. 'The Elders are very tired.'

Tim had forgotten that it was only because of the Elders that Percy was there with them.

'Percy, I won't see you ever again.'

The faint form of Percy shook his head, and tried to smile. Already they could see the sofa through his body.

'I wish you luck, Tim,' he managed to say. 'I am so glad to have met you.'

'And you, Percy, and you. And I do hope Beppo is going to be all right. Give my love to him, please, will you, Percy?'

'And all will be well . . .' Percy was no longer there. Tim looked at the spot where his friend had just been sitting, and a dreadful ache took hold of his throat. It was all over. All the questions he had wanted to ask would never be answered now. He would never know if Beppo got better. He would never see Percy again.

It was a long, sad silence for them all.

'It'll all be all right now, Tim,' Grandfather said gruffly. 'I'm positive. Now there won't be any more Tribaxin to poison the sea, they'll all be as right as rain.'

'Well, I just can't believe my own senses. I really can't,' the Professor said.

Tim gave a huge yawn. He had tried not to, but suddenly he wanted to yawn and yawn and never stop, he was so tired.

'Come on, my lad. Bed for you,' the Minister said crisply. 'There'll be plenty of time to talk things over tomorrow. I'll have one of the Ministry cars take you both home, but not until after lunch, so you try and stay in bed in the morning.'

The Professor was still sitting quietly, rubbing his chin and looking thoughtful.

'You know, that story about the dolphins was quite fascinating. Quite creepy, too.'

'Creepy? Not creepy, surely,' the Minister said.

'I mean, it's a credible myth. That's what makes it creepy—its similarity to one of our own.'

They all stood up, ready to go to bed. Tim did not understand what the Professor was saying.

'What myth? What do you mean?' he asked.

'Why, haven't you ever heard of the country that disappeared under the sea "between big lands", like Percy said. Haven't you ever heard of Atlantis?'

He put an arm round Tim's shoulder, and proceeded to explain all about it, as they slowly walked up the stairs together.